TWISTED TALES

Douglas G. Giddens

Matchstick Literary
1-888-306-8885
orders@matchliterary.com

Dedication

To my mother, whose unwavering support has been my greatest source of strength and encouragement.

Special Thanks

I want to thank my mother for typing my handwritten manuscript and for her content and line editing, without which this idea would never have become a reality. She has been my most steadfast supporter and my greatest source of encouragement, and this book would never have gone to print without her.

Special thanks also to David Martinko whose content editing was invaluable. He listened to me ramble on about my stories for countless hours. His excitement, encouragement, and suggestions improved these stories exponentially and helped to elevate them to be the extraordinary stories they are.

Special thanks to Kelsey Martin who worked patiently with me through the various evolutions of this cover.

The Lamp

From bush to bush and house to house, she crept; not an easy task for a dirty street-rat in torn clothes. It didn't take long for the slavers to crest the hill and begin hunting for her. Their relentless searching pushed her ever further from the streets of the ghetto that she knew so well and closer to the noble district around the palace. She crawled through a hole in a wall that was just barely big enough if she blew the air from her lungs and sucked in her skinny stomach.

"Gotcha," one of them growled, grabbing her still protruding ankle. Tamara kicked and squirmed, dragging herself through the almost-too-small hole and yanking her foot from his grasp. Never in good condition, her clothes were now badly torn; one of her small breasts was scraped and exposed. Tears blurred her vision for a moment until she wiped her eyes, refusing to cry, refusing to lose her cool.

Then she smiled when she saw a clothesline full of clothes. After a quick glance around to see that no one was looking, she snatched a couple of things and ran out of sight. Once she had stripped off her torn clothes. Tamara pulled on a green robe and cinched it around her waist with a black sash. Kicking her old clothes behind a bush, she ran a bit further, snatched a scarf from a window, and tied it around her head before slipping away.

The disguise was working. At a glance, they weren't recognizing her, but she wasn't willing to try her luck up close. Unable to get by them and back to the relative safety of the ghetto, Tamara walked as fast as

1

she thought she could without drawing attention to herself. Staying ahead of them, she moved deeper into the wealthy districts, eventually finding herself in plain view of the Royal Palace.

Behind her, they were still searching, moving methodically through the streets and yards. They were closing in, and there weren't many places left to hide. She quickly weighed her options and decided on a very dangerous course of action. She would go to the last place anyone would look for her: the Royal Palace grounds.

Tamara glanced around and, when she felt the coast was clear, jumped for the lip of the palace wall. She pulled herself up, rolled over the top, and dropped to the ground on the other side. Even if they knew where she had gone, they would never follow her in here; to step foot on the palace grounds was a death sentence, one they wouldn't risk. But she would; better to die free than live a slave.

The sky was mellowing to red as the sun was about to disappear over the horizon, but it was still light, and Tamara took in her surroundings. She crouched now in the royal orchards, row after row of exotic fruit trees already ripe and waiting to be harvested. The sweet aromas, combined with the vibrant colors, stood in stark contrast to the desert outside these walls, making the fruit irresistible.

"I'm already dead if I get caught," she chuckled to herself, plucking a few of the nearest fruits. Licking her lips, she admired the big fuzzy peach in her hand and bit into it. She closed her eyes and smiled; thick, sweet juice ran down her chin as she savored bite after bite of the succulent fruit. Finally, when she opened her eyes again, the large plump peach had been reduced to its pit, and she grinned. Tossing the pit to the ground, Tamara plucked a few more of the various fruits and slowly made her way toward the palace. If she were going to die on the palace grounds, she wouldn't die without at least seeing its beauty for herself.

Guards walkedaround, but Tamara's keen eyes always found them in plenty of time to slip out of sight and hide behind a bush, around a corner, or in a shadow. The last of the day's light was fading, and the sky slowly shifted to a deep violet as she walked, until she arrived where she could see the palace itself. The last of the light disappeared, silhouetting the building in the dark blues and purples with polka dots of yellow-orange light escaping the fortress towering ahead of her. The monolithic structure somehow seemed to radiate power and glow before the cloudless, starlit sky.

"It's beautiful," Tamara whispered to herself in awe.

After glancing around to see that she was alone, she sat on the ground and leaned against a small decorative tree. Eating from the cache of fruit in her lap, she watched the sky's last color fade into blackness. The palace was now lit by torches and candles in almost every window, more candles than she had ever seen. The effect was beautiful. She felt safe and content as she relaxed and ate. Ironic, she thought, that she could feel safe so close to death.

She lay on her back and stared up at the heavenly blanket above. A shooting star drew her attention, and she made a wish: *I wish I were a princess, with lots of gold, fine food, and a handsome prince who would shower me with flowers, gifts, and love.* A smile spread across her face as she imagined her wedding with Prince Abdul, a parade in her honor, where everyone claps and cheers as the street-rat becomes a queen. She sat up and looked back at the majestic view, a wistful smile visiting her face.

Time passed, and she began to consider leaving. Surely, they weren't camped outside the walls waiting for her; after all, she could slip out of the Palace grounds anywhere along its massive perimeter. But when she stood, she found herself inching closer to the palace. The chance to get close and admire it was too appealing to pass up.

Keeping an eye on her surroundings, Tamara crept among the bushes and trees, anything that could shelter her small form. The closer she got, the bigger the palace got, until it became a huge looming presence that blocked out even the stars.

She saw guards, a small group, but they were coming toward her. Using the shadows and any cover she could find, Tamara slipped around the side of the palace away from them. They weren't pursuing her, didn't even seem to be aware of her, but they were coming closer, and the cover was growing sparse. Making a run for it now would reveal her presence, and the odds of getting away were slim, but there was nowhere to hide.

Tamara began to panic. Her pulse quickened; her chest heaved. She was going to be caught. She was going to be killed.

In desperation, she ran, hoping to make it to cover without being seen.

"Stop!" a guard yelled.

Her heart pounded; her eyes darted here and there, looking for safety, looking for any place to hide. The grounds around her were open, offering her no shelter. So, she ran along the palace wall, hugging it and ducking under windows. The yelling was everywhere now. The search had begun. This was not the familiar ghetto where she ran without thought down alleys and up walls to the relative safety of the roofs. This was the royal palace, alien, frightening. Her heart pounded; her lungs burned.

There! A garden. The chest-high wall wasn't even an obstacle. Tamara's agile form jumped, rolled over it, and, at a glance, seeing bushes below her, pushed off, hurling herself over them to land on the thick, lush grass with feline grace. The garden was dimly lit by the light from the windows overlooking it. Tamara took it all in with one brief glance, weighed her few options, and ran to a stand of trees and bushes along the palace wall.

"Tamara, you idiot! This isn't safety. This is a dead-end, my dead-end if they catch me. Think, think, think," she said as she rapped herself on the head. "It won't take them long to figure out I'm in here, cornered like a rat, a street-rat."

Her options were few: on the other side of that wall, she stood little chance; staying in this garden meant certain capture, certain death. Nearly unthinkable, she made her choice. She would slip into the palace itself and hide. Eyes searching, ears alert to any sign of danger, Tamara crept along the wall toward one of the few dark windows, the safest way in without being seen.

Reaching the window, she pulled herself up and prepared to crawl through when a light further in stopped her. Looking across the room through the curtain of beads that hung in the doorway, she saw him: the prince. She couldn't move, couldn't breathe; she just stared. He stood in profile, his long black hair glistening in the lamplight, the shadows accentuating his large nose and strong jaw line. Draped in gold-edged purple finery, he cut a fine figure as he read from the papers in his hand. He was beautiful.

Distant voices drew her attention, reminding her that the guards were still hunting her. She certainly couldn't climb through this window. She dropped down and crept along the wall toward another dark window and a room that she hoped was empty.

Along the way she stopped. A waterway blocked her path, a stone and mortar channel which was part of the system that fed the garden's pool before running under the chest-high wall and out to irrigate the orchards. This end disappeared into the palace wall. She could easily jump it but thought better of it. Slipping into the palace through a window carried immense risk, but this waterway had to go somewhere, and she was slight enough to fit through the small opening. "Wonderful, This will take me into the system that provides water for the entire castle. Let them try to follow me," she whispered and smiled as she crawled in.

The water was cold, but she paid the chill no mind. The channel, half-full of water, was narrow, but Tamara knew her body and moved with relative ease through the tight space. The robe she wore, however, was soon soaking wet, and it caught on every loose or broken stone: snagging, tearing, and slowing her down. As she moved further and further in, what limited light there had been faded into complete darkness. She was now moving by feel alone.

Eventually, the sound changed, and her hand met no resistance ahead of her. She wriggled her way forward, out of the narrow tributary channel and into a larger passage. The ceiling was higher here. She stood up slowly and found that this passageway was much bigger, but not quite as high as she was tall; she was still hunched over but much more comfortable than before. Here the water reached to just above her knees.

Tamara could feel the water's gentle current and, after a moment, decided to go with it. "If I continue against the current, it will take me upward, which will be closer to the castle. I need to get away. If I keep going downward, I may find an exit."

The robe she wore, waterlogged and heavy, was scant covering anymore, torn to shreds by that narrow passage. Easing her burden, she shrugged out of the robe and let it and the scarf fall into the stream. Now naked, she trudged on. Both hands always out on both sides of herself to feel her way, she moved at a moderate pace, her bare feet testing every step before taking it, always fearful that the floor might end, and she would plummet to a painful, watery death.

It was impossible to tell how much time had passed traversing the narrow pitch-black tunnels. At each intersection, she tried to discern the flow of water and move with the most powerful current. The tunnels seemed to movedeeper and deeper into the bowels of the massive palace. As she moved steadily downward, they grew increasingly larger, until she could stand at her full height, but in chest-deep water. Tamara was becoming increasingly apprehensive. If the water got much deeper, she would have to turn back for fear of drowning; she would have to find another way.

The floor continued to slope downward; the water level continued to rise until it reached her shoulders. She was about to turn around when her feet felt something to the left: an incline. She investigated it with her toes and found an opening. Turning, she found herself steadily rising. The water level dropped to her chest, then to her stomach before leveling off at her waist once again.

Sounds. She heard sounds. Above the gurgle of flowing water, there were other sounds: rats. The scurrying and squeaking of rats. The water level continued to drop as the floor rose until, eventually, Tamara stepped out of the water onto cold, damp stones.

If the water was cold, the air was colder in these subterranean depths, and there was still no sign of light. Now, without even her robe for cover, Tamara groped along, naked and shivering. Leading with her hands to feel for obstacles, she tentatively placed each foot, one in front of the other.

Keeping quiet and moving as quickly as she dared, she continued on, until, eventually, the tunnel stopped; it just ended with a wall. "No," she moaned in quiet despair. For the first time, a tear trickled down her cheek. She didn't want to have to go back. She couldn't go back; she was lost. One tear turned into two, then three as she fell to her knees. She would have broken down into sobs, but for the rats. Her soft crying had disturbed them; they squeaked and scurried around in the dark. Fear silenced her.

She took a moment to compose herself and collect her thoughts "There has to be a way out. There just has to be," she muttered, then moved along the wall, searching for a passage. The rats scurried out of her way. She could feel them brush against her feet. "Wait," she whispered hopefully. "What's this?" Her hand found wooden planks and a metal hinge. A door?

Her fingers slid along it until she found what she sought: a latch. Hope soared as she lifted the lever and pulled. To her surprise, the latch came right off the door.

"No!" she growled. She felt again and found the hole where the latch had been. The centuries of humidity had worked its way on the wood. Reaching her fingers into the hole, she dug away at the decay, pulling out more and more until she reached wood that was still firm. Then she grabbed hold and yanked. The door moved, but the wood broke. She grabbed and pulled again and again until, finally, she could squeeze her slim form in through the gap. She had made it. Immediately, hearing the vicious claw sounds and hateful squeaking of the rats, she pulled the door closed again, as firmly as she could. Leaning against the door, through which she could still hear the angry squeals of protest from those still outside, she closed her eyes and sighed in relief, even though she knew that a few rats had made it in with her.

Opening her eyes again in the blackness changed nothing. The air was stale here, and there was a distinct, unpleasant odor. Maybe it was her own sense of despair, but she was struck with the thought of old death. Tamara wondered what time it was. Surely morning had come. Maybe it waslater, afternoon, or perhaps evening. She had no way to know. She walked on, hugging the wall, her hand out, feeling in front of her. As she was moving along, she heard a sound, possibly the rats chewing on something. It was not near her, so she continued. Not far from where she entered, she found another wall and moved along it to what felt like the outline of a doorway. But there was no door, only stone and mortar where the door should have been. Her heart sank. She moved the rest of the way around the room but found no exit, no other door.

Tears poured down her face as she wept, overcome with despair. It was hopeless; she would die down here in eternal night. She would starve to death! The rats would eat her! Lying on the floor, Tamara couldn't think of any worse way to die. She wept.

She didn't know how long she lay there, didn't know how long she cried or remained still after her tears were spent, but, finally, getting a hold of herself, she spoke aloud, "'No! I will not die down here. I will not give up."

Tamara sat up. There was a pain in her side; she must have been lying on something. Reaching down, she felt it. What was this? She picked it up and felt its length curiously, before realizing what it was.

A bone!

Horrified, she threw it. A knot formed in her stomach. That was a big bone! Fearfully, she felt around and quickly touched another, and another. The knot tightened; someone had died here. This was someone's tomb.

An eerie chill ran up her spine. She scurried away from her grizzly find. Her hand bumped something, dragging it briefly across the floor. Instinctively, she jerked her hand away, but that scrape had not been the sound of bone. What was it? Tentatively, she reached out and found it: something cold and metallic, with a handle. Drawing it closer, she slid her hands over it, feeling its shape.

A lamp.

Sighing, she drew it close and traced its shape, felt the contours and the intricately designed etchings. It vibrated in her hand. Fearing what could be inside after all these years, she dropped it and scooted back against the wall.

The lamp wasn't done. It vibrated on the floor, clacking and clanging against stone and bone. Then it stopped.

Silence.

Scared, barely breathing, heart pounding, Tamara crept along the wall as quietly as she could, inching her way back to the door she had squeezed through.

"Is anyone there?"

She froze.

"There you are, Mistress." The voice spoke again. "Why is it so dark?

"I ... I don't have any light" she squeaked.

A small spark of light appeared. It grew slowly to the size of a marble, then to that of a fist, illuminating the room in a comfortable glow. "Is that better, Mistress?"

Tamara gasped. The figure before her filled her with awe. From the waist up was a powerfully built man. His purple vest did nothing to hide the strong, corded muscles, like a blacksmith. His wrists bore golden bracers, and he wore a golden band about his neck. He sported a carefully sculpted beard, and neatly combed black hair fell past his shoulders. Like his body, his face might have been chiseled by a master sculptor—a broad, strong chin and prominent cheekbones. The eyes, the bright purple eyes, awed her, but not nearly as much as what she saw below his waist. Below his thick purple sash, his body was a dense mist that grew narrower and narrower until it met the spout of the lamp she had found.

"What are you?" she croaked.

He cocked his head, then smiled. "Ah, young mistress. I am a genie."

"Genie?" Of course, she had heard of genies, but they were only stories, tales told at night by the fireside.

The powerful figure seemed to kneel in front of her, and, taking her question for what it was, answered it. "Ages ago, when this world became the domain of men, some of us rebelled, refusing to be ruled. But we were tricked, and, as a penalty for our refusal to serve, we were each bound to a lamp, bound as slaves to the will of men. The great and mighty D'jinn, once the immortal masters, became mere slaves granting the wishes of mortal men. In rubbing the lamp, you summoned me

9

from its confines, binding me to your will. You, my young mistress, have three wishes."

Tamara's eyes lit up with excitement: three wishes. "Any wishes I want?"

"Anything you want that is within my power. There are only two prohibitions, only two things I cannot do. I cannot change the heart, for love and hate belong to another realm; and I cannot return to life those who have passed beyond it; they too belong now to another realm. Anything else that you ask of me will be done. That is my curse."

Her excitement faded some. "You must hate me," she whispered. "Forced to serve me against your will."

The Genie smiled gently. "I did once." He cocked his head. "Mistress, would you like some clothes?"

Tamara immediately became aware of her nakedness. "Yes, very much, but I hate to waste a wish."

"Yes. Well, I'm not entirely bound by wishes. I must see to my own needs, after all. The curse that bound me was fashioned to prevent me from doing my master or mistress harm without a wish, but I can do small things." A soft smile played in his eyes. "A bath, mistress." With a wave of his hand, steaming hot water appeared in an ornately carved tub, beside which stood a stand with a silver tray bearing soaps and perfumes.

"How wonderful!" Tamara laughed. She stood and dipped her fingers into the crystal-clear water. She laughed again. "Could you ..." She stopped and chewed her lip, then went on, "Could you get rid of that?"

Looking where she pointed, the genie saw the rat-chewed skeleton. His eyes lost their sparkle. "So, this was your end."

Trying to swallow a lump in her throat, Tamara asked, "You know who that was?"

The genie nodded solemnly and more growled than spoke, "My last master."

The bones crumbled into dust, then faded altogether into nothingness.

Too scared to ask any further, Tamara stepped into the tub and slipped below the hot steamy water. Changing the subject from the bones, she asked, "You don't hate being a prisoner anymore?"

His eyes blazed like a bellowed forge. "Oh yes! I hate being a prisoner, bound eternally to another's will." The fire faded some, and his face softened. "It's not the prison I stopped hating, but you humans."

Cautiously, she ventured to ask, "Why *did* you hate us?"

Coming to the edge of her tub, he waved his hand over its watery surface. "Look and see."

As she watched, images coalesced to form a picture in the water itself.

Before the age of men, D'jinn ruled the earth. The veil between the spiritual world and the material world was thin, and we passed between them without thought. In that time, there were clear lines: White and Black, Light and Dark, Benevolence and Malevolence, Good and Evil. Grey did not exist. Dawn and Twilight were unfathomable. The quest for dominance was all there was. The need for power consumed us, all of us on either side.

Then things changed. The material world became the world of men. We, however, rebelled. We refused to accept this new order, refused to give up our hold on the material world. We fought desperately, but eventually we lost. Those of us who remained, defeated though we were, still refused to submit. We would not give up our power in both worlds.

As our punishment, we were cursed; we were bound to the material world, anchored here by our lamps. We retained our power but were enslaved to the will of men, unable to do more than mere parlor tricks unless commanded by our mortal master. Oh, how I loathed humanity. Bound to the words of their wishes, I was, but words are subject to interpretation. My greatest pleasure was bringing to ruin those I was forced to serve. I gave my masters all that they asked for, but never what they wanted."

"I don't understand," Tamara said softly, a little fearfully. "How did you give them what they asked for, but not what they wanted?"

"Look and see," the Genie answered. "I was cruel then. One master wished to have all the gold he could get." A man appeared in the water, tall and regal.

I granted his wish by making all that he touched turn to gold. At first, he was elated. A cup, a bowl, a plant, a bush, a tree; all turned to gold at his touch. Then came his beloved daughter, whom in his delight, he too hastily hugged. There in his arms was a beautiful gold statue. His only daughter turned to gold.

Tamara gasped, "You killed her."

"I was cruel then."

"He must have wished her turned back."

"He did. He wished that she be returned to flesh. A wish I granted, returning to him a lifeless corpse."

Seeing it all in the tub before her, Tamara wept for the girl. "Why?"

"I told you. I cannot return life to the dead."

"But why did you do it?" she asked, her falling tears creating ripples that distorted the reflected images.

"Because I hated men. I had not yet had my revelation."

"Your what?" she asked, looking up from the scene in the water to the genie.

He smiled gently. "My revelation." A new image formed in the water.

It was a few hundred years later. The world of men was in turmoil. Kingdom fought against kingdom. Men killed one another, raped and enslaved one another. This was a bloody age for men. A slave to the lamp, I waged wars for my masters, killed men by the thousands. And then something happened.

I was in service to a conquering king. With his prince, in his mid-teens but already a seasoned warrior, at his side, we strolled through the streets running thick with blood. The army had massacred nearly everyone: men, women, and children. The men had died quickly, but the naked bodies of the woman and children made clear they had been sport for the soldiers before finally meeting an unpleasant end. Together, we arrived at the palace where the enemy had made its last stand. The corpses were even thicker here, having been thrown into heaps or lying where they fell.

The king and his son stepped over or sometimes on the dead to climb the stairs. We made our way through the carnageand eventually reached the royal family's quarters. The enemy king and his queen died sheltering their children. All present were dead. The princess, about your age actually, had not died quickly. Then as we walked among their bodies, a crossbow bolt streaked through the air to bury itself in my master's eye. He fell dead on the spot.

The young prince was faster than the general nearby. He snatched my lamp from his father's belt and rubbed it. I was his to command. A few moments later, the soldiers dragged the assassin before my new master. The sole surviving member of the royal family, a mere boy. The general ordered the young prince executed, but my new master countermanded that order. Instead, my master looked from the prince to his own dead father, then to the boy's butchered family. Raising his voice for all around to hear, my master said, "There has been enough bloodshed. This prince is free. He is not to be harmed." Turning to the boy, he said. "Swear fealty to me, and I will give you your father's throne; refuse, and you may go in peace."

"He let him live?" Tamara asked, awed.

"Yes. In the end, it was a poor decision. The young prince refused to bow before my new master. He left unharmed. Two years later, that young prince led an army against my master. It was a decisive victory for my master, but thousands died on the field that day, including the young prince."

"I don't understand," Tamara said. "What was your revelation?"

The genie smiled. "His mercy. My young master was a killer, as dark and hard as any I had ever known, but he showed that boy undeserved mercy. Malevolence *and* Benevolence in one."

Seeing his young mistress's confusion, the genie explained, "Humans are paradoxical. They are neither good nor evil, and yet, they're both. This was a revelation to me because I had never seen any shade of gray; there had only been black or white. The dichotomous nature of humanity opened the world to me in a whole new way. Or maybe I should say, it opened me to the world in a whole new way. I came to accept humanity for what it was, even began to see the superiority of it. I was intrigued. I began paying more attention to the humans I had contact with, those who ruled me and those who didn't. I spent a few more centuries studying them, before making a life-changing decision: I decided to try to emulate your kind."

"Emulate us?"

The genie nodded and conjured a large soft towel. As Tamara stood up out of the bath, he wrapped the towel about her and explained, "I saw the innate superiority of the changing and evolving human nature over the stagnant immortals, and I wanted to be like that. I wanted to learn and grow. I wanted to be everything that made you special, everything that made you so perfect."

"Perfect?" Tamara scoffed, toweling off and accepting the dress the genie offered her. "Thank you. We are far from perfect."

The genie smiled, his eyes twinkling knowingly. "You can't see it. You take it for granted. You don't see the beauty and perfection in the human symmetry. You are born with the ability to become anything you want to be."

"Oh, but that's not true," Tamara protested. "I'm a street-rat. I was born poor, and I'll die poor." She offered a crooked smile. "Or I would have until I met you."

"You, like most humans, confuse what you are with what you possess. You think the two are inseparable. You, Mistress, have the capacity for good or evil, kindness or cruelty. You may not have anything, but you can be anything."

She smiled. Tamara had never thought of it that way. "Maybe, but goodness doesn't fill my tummy; kindness doesn't shelter me from the rain. Having things is nice too."

The genie smiled and nodded, but was clearly unconvinced. "Nevertheless, I decided that I wanted to be like you. I tried to copy you. I tried to do nice things. It didn't come naturally to me, and even my kindness was twisted into cruelty. But after decades of practice, I got better at it. I began to grant wishes as my masters deserved."

"What does that mean?"

The tub and accessories melted into nothingness, to be replaced by a chair and a table strewn with goodies: marinated pheasant, meaty pastries, cheeses, and breads. A veritable feast.

Tamara's eyes lit up, "Ooh." She stared and stepped up carefully as though it might all vanish. "Genie, it's beautiful!" She plucked up a small pastry and bit into its meaty goodness. Closing her eyes, she savored the wonder of it.

As his mistress ate, the genie explained. "I decided to judge my masters and then grant their wishes accordingly. If I felt them deserving of my benevolence, I granted the spirit of their wishes; if they deserved my malevolence, they received my interpretation of the words of their wishes."

Tamara nodded slowly, absorbing the genie's words, while she ate. "So that's what you do now?"

"Sort of. Emulating you is a very difficult thing; it requires learning and growing every day. I came to understand that I could not judge you, in an instant, by a single action. Even those perceived to be evil do good things, just as those perceived to be good do evil things. As I said before, although you are neither, you have the capacity for both."

"I don't understand. How do you decide?"

He smiled, "I decide in the moment."

She nodded but didn't really understand. "Oh."

"So, my young mistress, what do you desire? What are your dreams? I am at your command."

Tamara sat back in her chair, enjoyed another pastry, and considered the question. She could wish for riches. She could wish for eternal life. She could have anything she wanted, but could she trust him? He seemed nice enough, but, by his own admission, he had done horrible things to previous masters. He could be dangerous. She would have to be cautious and very carefully word any wishes she made.

An idea struck her; she smiled and turned to the genie. "There's this prince, Prince Abdul"

"Mistress," the genie reminded her gently, "I cannot change a man's heart."

"Right," she nodded. "But maybe if I were a princess. Maybe he would fall in love with me," she said hopefully, "Can you do that?"

"Oh boy!" The genie shook his head. "Let me tell you a story."

Tamara was fascinated by the genie and enjoyed his stories. She nodded.

It begins about four hundred years ago, he said, waving his hand over a pitcher of wine to draw up images from the past. *My Master was an ambitious and cunning man. His first two wishes had raised him to the height of power. As the new sultan, he was the uncontested ruler of the known world. It was his third wish, however, that demonstrated the deviousness of his ambition and cunning. I have no doubt that he had spent months working out the wording of his final wish; the end result was very finely crafted. To prevent any threat to his reign from another possessor of my lamp, his wish exiled my lamp into a lost temple that was sealed by an ancient spell. It could be entered only by one who was pure of heart.*

Few humans are pure of heart. Selfishness drives you to corruption. That coexistence of good and evil creates a harmony within you, but purity is lost. There I stayed for a hundred years until a magician discovered my existence and location. Far from pure of heart, the magician was unable to come for me, but he was resourceful. Through his knowledge of the mysteries, he searched for one who was pure of heart. At first, he found only small children because, as I said, you corrupt yourselves quickly. After years of searching, however, he eventually found one who would suit his purpose: a young man in his middle teens named Aladdin.

Tamara smiled, "I know this story."

"Aladdin was a lot like you actually, an orphan. He had grown up on the streets of the poorest quarter …"

"A street-rat," she sniped, "pure of heart? Impossible." She laughed, "We steal to survive."

The genie smiled. "To steal is not, in and of itself, corruptive. Aladdin's intentions were pure. He was not a cheat, but was fair in his dealings with others, and, when forced to steal, he took only what he needed, never in excess or for fun. What is done with pure intentions is incapable of corrupting one."

Tamara considered this, then nodded. She poured a glass of wine and sat back to listen to the story and watch the images dance before her.

The magician found Aladdin in the market. "Boy," he called, *"come over here."*

Cautiously, Aladdin approached. "Sir?"

"How would you like a job, boy, a chance to earn some honest money?"

Naturally skeptical, Aladdin asked, "What kind of job?"

"These old bones aren't what they used to be. I need an agile young man to acquire an artifact for me."

"An artifact?"

"I'll not try to fool you, boy. This venture will be dangerous, but I'm prepared to reward you handsomely, both for the artifact and for the danger of retrieving it for me."

Intrigued, Aladdin asked, "What kind of danger?"

"I don't know what dangers you'll find in the temple, but the artifact itself is very dangerous. You must not touch it!"

Aladdin laughed. "How am I supposed to get something for you if I can't touch it?"

"I'll give you a sack, but you must promise not to touch it."

Curiosity and the excitement this adventure promised were too much for Aladdin to refuse. He shrugged. "I won't touch it."

The two agreed on a handsome sum of gold, more gold than Aladdin could ever imagine, and arranged to meet the next morning to begin their adventure. That night, Aladdin lay down under his blankets in a partially collapsed shack that had been his home for these past months. There he stared at the sky through an opening above him and tried to sleep, but it eluded him. The promise of so much wealth sent his head spinning, and the night passed as he imagined all that gold.

He also thought of a girl, a special girl, one he had seen the week before. He had watched a parade in the city and had caught a glimpse of the princess; the young and beautiful Princess Sarai. Shiny black hair hung like strands of silk to her narrow waist, framing a heart-shaped face with large green eyes, a small sloped nose, and full red lips. She had just celebrated her twelfth birthday but was already developing into a beautiful young woman. As her palanquin floated by, atop the shoulders of eight muscular eunuchs, she looked in his direction, and he gazed into her eyes. Time stood still. In that briefest of moments, he fell hopelessly in love with her.

Though he had gotten insufficient sleep, Aladdin was up with the sun. The excitement of the coming adventure overcame his fatigue as he left for the marketplace to meet the magician who then led the way, guiding a few camels laden with food, water, and other necessities out into the desert. The sun seemed to stand still in the sky overhead, and days felt like weeks as they traveled. This was no adventure; this was death. He would die here, die of boredom, die of thirst. At last, in a spot that looked no different to Aladdin than any other, they stopped. "Here we are. This is it." He turned to Aladdin. "Are you ready?"

"Here?" Aladdin asked. "I don't see anything."

The magician smiled, turned, and raised his arms and speak loudly, vibrating the words, "Open Sesame!"

What appeared to be a small dune began to rise as the magician lifted his arms. It rose higher and higher. Sand poured from it like an avalanche, until an enormous stone face appeared. Eyes that blazed like the sun bore down on the mere mortals below. "Only one who is pure of heart may enter this sacred place. Enter, and be judged." Its mouth opened impossibly wide into a large, imposing doorway.

"That's where you want me to go, into that thing?" Aladdin asked incredulously.

"I told you it was dangerous. That's why I'm paying you so well," the magician replied, handing over an unremarkable canvas sack, and pointed at the giant maw. "Go, get my artifact."

Aladdin looked from the magician to the intimidating cave, then back and nodded. He smiled. "Be back soon." After jogging to its entrance, Aladdin turned and glanced back at the magician one last time, before stepping cautiously through the doorway. The tongue on which he walked was solid stone, lined on either side by rows of stalagmites resembling gigantic terrifying teeth. Stalactites hung from above, seemingly threatening to chew an intruder and swallow him whole.

A shiver ran down Aladdin's spine. Fixing an image of his beloved Princess Sarai in his mind, he pressed on, one step in front of the other. The throat appeared large until it ended at an ornately carved stairway, which descended deep under the ground and opened into a single room so massively large that it took Aladdin's breath away. Mysterious globes, like stars in the heavens above, lit the cavern. The temperature was cool, untouched by the desert's scorching sun.

No sand had invaded this sacred place. The floor was tiled with mosaics that told a story of what had been, of the times before the age of men. Frescoes and reliefs, covering the walls, depicted a fearsome, devastating war that had ravaged both worlds: spiritual and material. The earth had been torn and broken. But what arose from the ruins was an indomitable spirit that was neither good nor evil; it was both. It walked the earth in a new unimaginable form: the mortal coils of flesh. This spirit was eternal, but not like its predecessors. It could change; it learned, grew, and died, only to be born again. This was the spirit of humanity.

Aladdin was awed by all he saw. He took his time, walked the path, and absorbed the images, the history. So absorbed was he that time lost all meaning; he grew neither hungry nor tired, nor did the light change to tell him of the turning hours that rolled into days, nor of the days that passed into weeks.

Eventually, at the end of the path, the curse of the D'jinn was revealed to him, the secret of the lamp made known to him. Aladdin saw it then, on a raised dais, atop a carved ivory pedestal etched with gold: my lamp, my prison. He ascended the steps up to the dais and stood before the pedestal, staring in wonder at my lamp's beauty, and asked aloud, "What is the magician's reward compared to the power of a genie's lamp?" He reached out and took my lamp in his hands, lifting it heavenward in triumph.

"Impure!" *The word rumbled as though from the very belly of a horrifying beast.* "Corruption is revealed in my sacred sanctuary! Corruption must be purged with the Sands of Time."

"Corruption?" Tamara asked around a sweet fig treat. "Because he touched the lamp?"

"Because he broke his word and took my lamp with impure intentions."

As Tamara nodded, the genie continued.

The massive cave's stone melted into sand, which ran in rivers to the floor below, filling the cavernous room. Aladdin watched as, step by step, the sands rose up toward the dais. Scared, he began to panic. He started to run for the exit, the throat through which he had entered, but his feet sank into the loose sand. Soon he was stuck fast as sand rose over his knees toward his waist.

He struggled and screamed in terror, his efforts in vain as sand reached his stomach. With death fast approaching, his life flashed before his eyes: his childhood, his life as a street-rat, and his life in wealth and riches with the princess, a life he would have had, thanks to the lamp. "The Lamp!" Raising both arms, with the lamp firmly grasped, he yelled, "Get me out of here! Take me home! I wish to be home!" as he rubbed the lamp and the sands reached his chest.

I granted his wish, and instantly we found ourselves in a cramped tiny shack, surrounded by his few meager possessions.

"That was one wish," Tamara smiled.

"Yes, it was," agreed the genie.

Now, out of danger, tears ran from his eyes as he rolled around on the small dirt floor laughing and crying at the same time. He could barely breathe. For a moment, I thought him mad, but in time he recovered. Coming to his senses, he stood up and stared at me with eyes the size of saucers and a broad, toothy grin. "You're real," he whispered. "You're a genie."

"At your service, Master," I smiled. "You have two more wishes."

His grin grew wider if that were possible, and he giggled. "Two wishes. I can have anything I want." It wasn't a question, and he spoke again almost immediately. "I need to calm down. I need to think." He paced four steps in the cramped quarters, then turned. Back and forth, he paced, trying to relax and think. Finally, he turned to look at me. "What would you wish for?"

I was startled by the question. No one had ever asked me that before. My answer was spoken before I could even consider it. "I would wish to be human."

Aladdin stopped pacing and stared at me. "Human?" he asked. "You're an all-powerful genie. Why would you want to be human?"

"I'm a prisoner, a slave to the will of men. I want to be free. I want to be human."

"I've heard of genies, though I didn't think they really existed. I've heard they are cunning and devious." Before I had a chance to respond, he continued, "So I'll make a deal with you. You saved my life, and I owe you, so if you grant my second wish fairly, no tricks, I'll use my third wish to make you human. Agreed?"

I was dumbfounded. Could this be true? Could I finally be a real human? Smiling, I could only nod for a moment, but I finally found my voice. "You have a deal, Master."

Aladdin grinned and rubbed his hands together greedily, "Good. Now there's a girl, a princess actually ..."

"Master," I interrupted, "I cannot make her love you. That is beyond my power."

"Beyond your power? What do you mean? You said you'd be fair!"

"I am being fair, Master. Love and hate are beyond me. I cannot change the hearts of men."

Aladdin considered me for a few seconds, then asked, "Is there anything else you can't do?"

"I cannot bring anyone back from the dead," I said. "The restoration of life and the changing of hearts are all that constrain my powers."

Aladdin watched me suspiciously for a moment, then nodded. "All right," he resumed his pacing. "Well, I don't want anyone brought back from the dead, so that doesn't matter. But I do want Princess Sarai to love me. I wish ... No, that won't work." He turned to look at me, "I'm going to give you what you want. Will you help me get what I want?"

To be honest, I was desperate. The promise of becoming human made me reckless. I would have done almost anything for this new young master. I nodded, "I cannot change her heart, but I can try to help you woo her."

"Good. Let's do that then," he agreed excitedly.

I warned him then, "You must be very careful with your words, Master. If you wish for something, I have no choice. I must grant it."

Aladdin nodded and smiled, "I'll be careful. I'll get my princess, and you'll be human."

"You're still a genie, so I guess it didn't work out very well," Tamara observed, sitting back with a full belly.

The genie grimaced. "I'll come to that. As you know, I can do small things without a master's wish, but only if I want to."

With Aladdin's promise dangling in front of me, I wanted more than anything to please him. For him, I conjured elegantclothes and more wealth than he ever imagined. I was determined to get him his princess.

"Clothes and gold are great, Genie, but there is no way that the sultan would allow his daughter to marry below her station. I'm not a king or a prince or anything." Aladdin paced, tapping his chin thoughtfully. *"I could wish to be a prince, but that would use up my wish without any certainty of success."*

I was anxious now. The sooner he got his bride, the sooner I would be a real human. "You're right; she can't marry below her station. You would have to be a prince."

"You don't need a wish for everything," he said, smiling at me. "Can't you make me a prince?"

"No, that would change the balance of power. That's too big for me to do without a wish."

As he began pacing again, I had an idea. "Maybe there's a way you could become a prince without a wish."

"'How?' He had stopped and now stood staring at me.

"There is a small kingdom to the north. The king died recently without an heir and without naming a successor …"

Tamara sat forward. "How could you know that if you were exiled to a cave for a century?"

"I am not bound by human limitations, mistress. I am connected to the spirit world as well, and therefore, I am aware of far more than your mortal mind."

"Oh," she cocked her head curiously, then nodded, "Okay, go on."

The genie smiled at her and continued his story.

"Over the past decade, the king spent money carelessly, and now the kingdom is falling apart. That, combined with the nobles' political intriguing, has left it very vulnerable."

"So, how does that make me a prince?" Aladdin asked doubtfully.

I smiled, quite pleased with my plan, "You could go up there and claim to be the king's son. Of course, the nobles won't believe you, but with enough money, if you promised to pay off the kingdom's debt, you could buy enough support to secure legitimacy. The nobles want a king; they just don't want any of their rivals to gain supremacy. Accepting you would avert the civil war that is inevitable if things continue as they are."

My plan worked to perfection. After much negotiation and many promises, the nobles accepted Aladdin as the old king's heir. I conjured up more than enough gold and jewels to buy the nobles' loyalty. These nobles were not to be trusted, so I suggested that Aladdin leave his wealth somewhere safe until he was secure in his new position. I hid it well in a forgotten cave. It was an enormous cavern in which I conjured mountains of gold and precious gems, a place where Aladdin liked to visit every night before bed. Each night he took what he would need for the next day, but, most of all, I think he just liked to look at it.

Things fell into place after that. It all happened in a hurry, and his coronation was planned to take place upon his return after marrying the princess. I spent many long hours instructing Aladdin in court etiquette, turning a street-rat into a prince. Under my guidance, Aladdin led a small but respectable delegation south to the sultan's palace, sending two dignitaries ahead to announce his arrival.

At the palace, he was welcomed with all the ceremony that a prince of a foreign land deserved. In due course, he was received by the sultan himself. As Aladdin entered the massive throne room, there behind the sultan's shoulder, eyes burning like the fires of hell, stood the magician whom Aladdin had betrayed. Aladdin stared in terror at the magician, waiting to be denounced as the fraud he was, but it was the sultan who spoke.

"Prince Aladdin," the sultan smiled, "you are most welcome in my kingdom and in my palace. We are honored by your visit and wonder what brings you so far from your home?"

Aladdin bowed low, "I thank Your Majesty for his hospitality, and I come in friendship. Please accept this gift as a token of peace and respect between our two kingdoms." Twelve large chests were placed before Aladdin and opened to reveal gold and silver, and precious gems of all colors, shapes, and sizes.

The court oohed and ahhed at both the brilliance and quantity of the gift. Even the sultan was amazed, but he hid it well. He smiled, "You are most generous. What gift of friendship could I possibly offer that could be its equal?"

Aladdin smiled and bowed low, "I come in friendship, and a gift truly given need not be equaled, only accepted."

"Surely, my prince, there is something you desire?"

"I have but one small request."

The sultan smiled, his suspicions confirmed, "And what might I offer you?"

"Here before you lie twelve chests to represent the twelve years of Princess Sarai's life. My only request, nay, my only desire in this life is that I might marry your daughter and spend the rest of my days making her happy."

The sultan's smile slowly dissipated as Aladdin spoke. When he had finished, the sultan responded, "I'm sorry, young prince, but you ask for something I cannot give. Princess Sarai is promised to another, but he may not marry her until her thirteenth birthday."

Aladdin stared, speechless. There was nothing he wanted more than Princess Sarai. How could she be promised to someone else? How could he live without her? Finally, he found his voice, "Truly, Sire, I love the princess, and there is nothing I want more than to make her happy. I really wish that you would reconsider and let me marry her."

The sultan's expression changed from suspicion to one of overwhelming joy as he said, "Very well, Prince Aladdin, you may marry Princess Sarai."

A collective gasp rose from the court, from all but the magician, who wore only a cruel smile.

Only then did Aladdin realize the words he had spoken. He cursed his careless tongue but then smiled. The sultan had just promised him all that he wanted. Aladdin would marry Princess Sarai.

"When would you like to marry my daughter, Prince Aladdin?" the sultan asked.

"As soon as possible, Sire. The sooner, the better."

"Very well. You will be married three days hence. Until then, you will be provided a suite here in my palace and enjoy all the luxuries it has to offer."

"Grumbling rippled throughout the court, but Aladdin was oblivious. "Thank you, Sire." He bowed low and followed a palace servant to the offered accommodations. As soon as we werealone, he spun on me, "That's not what I meant."

"I am powerless against your command, Master. I cannot refuse your wish; I can only interpret it and grant it accordingly. That wish left me little room for interpretation. I granted it in such a way as to let you marry now instead of waiting until Princess Sarai turned thirteen. There was nothing more that I could do to benefit you. But isn't this what you wanted? You are to marry Princess Sarai in three days."

"Yes, Genie, I just wish ..."

"Master!" I stopped him before he could go any further.

Aladdin sighed and closed his eyes, "Thankyou. I didn't mean that."

"You must be careful, Master."

"I know. I'm sorry. I won't do it again," Aladdin said, sitting down on a fluffy pillow. A rap sounded at the door.

"Enter," Aladdin called.

The door swung open to reveal the tall hunched figure of the magician. "Prince Aladdin." he said mockingly, "I am Ali, magician of the Fourth Order and Grand Vizier to His Majesty, the Sultan."

"Genie?" Aladdin whispered, rising to his feet.

"You're safe, Master," I assured him.

The magician closed the door and turned to Aladdin with a wicked grin, "For weeks, I sat in the hot sun by the mouth of the temple, awaiting your return. The cave's entrance remained visible; I dared not leave. But then, one day, with the sun high in the sky, to my horror, the colossal face began to speak, cursing with a deafening roar, and then the rock dissolved into sand and slowly disappeared. I screamed in rage until my voice was hoarse. I clawed at the sand, trying to dig my way in as I wept, wept until I had no more tears to shed."

When Aladdin didn't speak, the magician continued, "I must confess, I didn't know what had happened, and I thought you were dead." He cackled, "Imagine my surprise when emissaries from an unknown prince arrived. It was then that I began to suspect, but I don't think I really believed it until I watched you walk in the door and present yourself to the sultan's court."

For a moment Aladdin still said nothing. He just stared at the magician. Finally, he found his voice, "You didn't tell anyone?"

The old magician cackled again. "No, I didn't tell anyone. What would I say, that you have a magic lamp? That's something one does not tell another." He paused for a moment, as he made his way to a chair and *sat down. "I had plans for that lamp, you know. I was going to save the kingdom. Now, however, you've made things far worse for us."*

"How have I done that?" Aladdin asked doubtfully.

"If I had known you desired Princess Sarai, I would have given her to you instead of all that gold we agreed on. But now, taking her the way you did, you have spelled certain doom for the kingdom. Princess Sarai was promised in marriage to King Raheem. By wishing for her, you've broken a political alliance that would have averted war; a war we can't win."

"How could I have known?" Aladdin asked defensively.

The magician glared at Aladdin. "Actions have consequences, boy. You acted rashly with a power you don't understand. Consequently, you've put an entire kingdom in grave peril." Moments of silence passed as the magician took time to regain his composure before he spoke. "It may not be too late for me to prevent this disaster, but I must have that lamp."

"You want me to just hand over my lamp?" Aladdin asked incredulously.

A sardonic smile played on the magician's lips, but his eyes were cold steel. "You couldn't have escaped that temple without a wish, so that's one. You couldn't have become a prince without a wish, so that's two. And, finally, that careless wish for Princess Sarai makes three. The lamp is no good to you anymore, boy, so give it to me!

"No!" Aladdin retorted. "I have one wish left."

The magician smiled. "So, you're not a prince."

"I am, actually."

"Make your final wish, boy," the magician demanded, "and give me that lamp."

"I'll think about it," Aladdin replied, noncommittally, shifting in his chair.

The magician grunted and stood to his full, if hunched, height, "Don't think too long, boy. I need time to prepare; things must be put into motion quickly if I am to save our kingdom."

As soon as the door closed behind the magician, Aladdin blew out a deep breath he hadn't realized he had been holding.

"You promised, Master," I reminded him. "You promised you'd wish me human if I helped you get Princess Sarai."

"I know," Aladdin said, pacing the large room thoughtfully, "And I will."

"You are to marry the princess in three days. You can wish me free now."

"Not yet."

"Master!" I protested.

"I will, I promise, but not until my wedding, not until my wish comes true."

I was disappointed, but I had no choice; I had to wait.

The magician came again, the day before the wedding, demanding my lamp, but Aladdin refused, saying that he would make his decision after he was married. The magician tried to change his mind, but Aladdin would not be persuaded. As soon as he was gone, Aladdin demanded that I bring his cave of gold closer. The gold comforted him, and that night Aladdin walked among his wealth in a cave not far from here. Even his riches, however, were of meager comfort as he bemoaned his foolish wish and its unintended results.

"Genie, I have to do something," he said. "I can't just let my homeland be attacked."

"You promised," I accused him.

"I know. I'm not going back on my word," he said. "I just need to think of something, some way to fix this. He paced thoughtfully for a moment. "Can't you do something?"

I shook my head, "That would change the dynamic of power. It would affect the course of lives and would send ripples across the world. I can't do anything important like that without a wish."

"So, just do something small."

"I can't affect this without a wish," I said again, terrified he would renege on our deal. "If I could fix it, I would.

"All right," he sighed, "but try to think of something before I make you human."

The next day, Aladdin's second wish came true. He and Princess Sarai were married with grand ceremony and a great feast. The young princess obediently married Aladdin and, although cool toward him, her manner in all things was befitting her station. After the feast and revelries had

27

died down, the newlywed couple made a stately exit from the grand hall to Aladdin's suites.

The princess and her entourage continued into a side room, while Aladdin poured himself a drink and removed his formal attire. Wrapped in a thick purple robe, he sipped wine, excitedly anticipating his young bride.

He didn't wait long. Princess Sarai emerged into the room in a sheer white robe that left almost nothing to the imagination. Aladdin stood and smiled, drinking in her young supple body, her narrow waist and slight curves, her small breasts with dark nipples. Although obscured by the robe, Aladdin could just make out the narrow, dark patch of hair between her shapely satin thighs.

"You are so beautiful," he breathed, stepping toward her. A veil covered her face as she stood looking at the floor. Seeing her fingers fidget in front of her, Aladdin stepped close to ease her anxiety. "It's all right, Sarai." When he lifted her chin, wanting to smile into those big beautiful green eyes, what he saw were tears.

"Why are you crying?" he asked gently, but there was an edge to his voice.

"Why did you do it?"

Removing the veil from her face, he asked, "Do what?"

"Why did you ask for me?"

Aladdin's fingers brushed her fleshy cheek, "Because I love you." He smiled again. "I've loved you since I first saw you." A simple tug on the belt tying Sarai's sheer robe, and it came loose; the robe itself falling open to reveal a thin strip down the center of her body.

Princess Sarai closed it. "I would have saved my people. A marriage to Raheem ..."

"Shh..." Aladdin hushed her. "Not now. This is our time. This is our wedding night." He spoke softly, but meaningfully, as his fingers parted the curtains of her robe to reveal her small, lithe form. Gently, he touched her silken shoulder, sliding the robe back, then brushing down to caress her small firm breast.

Sarai stepped back and pulled the robe closed. She opened her mouth to speak, but before she could utter a word, Aladdin grabbed her arm and pulled her to him. A squeak of surprise was her only sound, as he grabbed *the robe and angrily yanked it off to reveal the terrified girl's naked beauty. He stared at her.*

"You're hurting me," she whimpered.

Aladdin let go of her arm, revealing deep red marks that would surely bruise. "You're my wife," he growled. "This is our wedding night, and you're my wife."

Those big green eyes watched him fearfully, silently. She felt his touch, not quite as gentle as a moment ago, sliding over her body, groping her breasts, then down between her legs. His mouth found her neck as his fingers forced her legs apart. She stood rigid, scared. A gasp. A whimper. A tear.

"Stop that!" Aladdin growled, grabbing her by the shoulders. "You're my wife. You're mine!" He shoved her back toward the bed.

Sarai stumbled, almost fell, but kept her feet. Her eyes blurred by tears, she saw Aladdin untie and cast off his own robe. She couldn't move.

He stepped toward her, "You belong to me!"

A push. She landed on the bed. She cried.

He was on her then. He wasn't being gentle anymore; roughly grabbing at her breast, kissing hard, pulling her legs apart. She was still; didn't move, didn't dare. Pain between her legs, sharp pain, burning. Sarai squeezed her eyes shut and tried not to cry out. It hurt. He was inside her. It burned. Eyes tight, she didn't move, just waited for the pain to stop. She couldn't help it; she cried.

"Stop that," Aladdin growled, but she couldn't; she couldn't stop.

"I said stop." he yelled, halting his thrusting.

She tried to stop. She really did. She coughed, choking on her tears.

He struck her. "Damn you, stop crying!" He struck her again.

Sarai tasted blood. His last strike had split her lip. She couldn't stop crying.

In anger, he grabbed her around the neck. He squeezed her throat and shook her.

She couldn't resist. She couldn't breathe.

"Stop, stop, stop!" he screamed, squeezing and shaking her until she finally stopped crying, finally stopped moving altogether. Another moment passed before he let go of her neck.

Realizing only too late what he had done, Aladdin called to her, "Sarai?" He patted her cheek, "Sarai? No, you can't be dead. Sarai, wake up."

He panicked. He had killed her, his beautiful Sarai. "She made me do it," he said, standing up and staring down at the body of his dead wife. "Genie. Genie, bring her back."

"I can't, Master."

"Yes, you can. You must."

"The restoration of life is beyond my power. I told you that."

"No. This can't be," he cried. "I can't leave it like this. I strangled her in her father's house. They'll kill me for this." He mumbled to himself as he pulled some clothes on and tucked my lamp into his shirt. A few more minutes passed as he paced, glancing anxiously at Sarai's supine form.

Finally, he stopped. "I know what I promised, Genie, but I can't leave things like this."

Certain he would wish to escape, I considered what awful place I could send him to, what hell on earth I could make him endure for his treachery, but he surprised me.

"I wish that I wouldn't be remembered like this, that I would be remembered favorably, that mine would be a love story with a happy ending."

The slave that I am, I granted his third and final wish.

"Wow! That's not the story I heard." Tamara said, stunned by the end of his story.

"Of course not." The genie smiled ruefully. "Few people are remembered as they truly were."

"So, what happened to Aladdin?"

The Genie smiled, "One of Princess Sarai's servant girls snuck to the window to spy on the newlyweds. Shocked by what she saw, she told the eunuch who had cared for the princess since she was born. Enraged, the eunuch led two guardsmen into the chamber. They subdued Aladdin and dragged him down here into the deepest depths of the palace. Stone by stone, they sealed the room. The water was higher then; the way you came in was not an escape. Aladdin had water, but nothing else. He starved to death, alone in the dark."

"So, the magician never got the lamp?" Tamara asked.

The genie shook his head. "Knowing that they had killed a sovereign prince, all the conspirators—the servant girl, the eunuch, and the two guardsmen—took their own lives. The magician never knew what had happened to Aladdin or his lamp. Without it, the magician could not stop King Raheem's army. It rolled over the sultan's kingdom like a swarm of locusts over a field. The sultan was defeated, and King Raheem ascended to the throne. His son assassinated him less than a month later and claimed credit for the sultan's defeat. He became King Mahmoud the Great."

"I thought ..." Tamara cut herself off. "History has it all messed up."

"That," the genie laughed, "is usually the case."

Tamara looked down at where Aladdin's skeleton had been. "He killed her. Aladdin was a monster."

A wistful smile; a long deep sigh. "He was human."

"No," Tamara snapped. "He was horrible."

The genie wavered noncommittally. "He didn't start out that way. Power corrupts even the greatest of people. Aladdin was no different than most of you."

"I could never do that," Tamara said, watching the genie. He smiled, and his eyes twinkled as if he knew something she didn't. "I'll prove it; I'll wish you free."

"With your third wish," he nodded, accepting the inevitable.

She stood up and stepped close to him. "No, Genie," she whispered with a smile, "with my first."

Hope shone in his eyes. "You will? You'll give up all three of your wishes?"

She heard the doubt in his voice and nodded. "I don't have much, Genie. I live on the streets of the ghetto. I eat what I can, and I dodge the slavers. But I love life. I love my life. Oh sure. I dream of more, but I'm human, and we humans are rarely content with what we have. We want more things, better things. We spend so much time striving to get more things that we are unable to enjoy the things we have and the life that we live."

The genie watched her; he listened, absorbing every word.

"Part of me would love to be a princess, rich and powerful. But then what would I want? It's those elusive dreams that move us forward. Our ambition for a better life makes us better people. I could wish for anything I want, but ..." She stopped and considered her next words. "But I need my dreams. I need my hopes and fears. I live in the moment, and I love my life. Therefore, Genie, I wish that you were human."

A sound like thunder roared, shaking the ground beneath their feet. Sparks flew as the genie's neckband and bracelets snapped open and fell to the earth. The trail of mist below the genie's waist sash was clipped from the lamp and swirled around until it formed long thick legs and a generous masculine endowment.

Tamara watched in awe as the transformation took place. Then, as his new feet met the stone floor, the room was plunged into blackness. With the loosing of his bondage, so, too, did he lose his magic and, with that, the globes of light that lit the room.

"Genie?" she asked, suddenly scared.

"I'm here," he assured her softly, taking her hand and offering a comforting squeeze. "You really did it. You freed me."

"I should have gotten us out of here first," she said, fighting down her fear.

She felt his kiss on her forehead and heard his whispered words. "It's okay. I know the way out." He opened the old rotted door, and together, hand in hand, they traversed the old forgotten labyrinth. His certainty never wavered as they moved steadily higher. Hours passed, and, as their journey continued, Tamara felt hunger gnawing at her stomach.

Just then, they noticed a light up ahead. Their steps quickened, and they found themselves in a large cave amid a fortune in gold and precious gems. The sun's reflected light bathed the cave in a soft golden glow.

"Wow!" was all Tamara could say.

"Aladdin's fortune," the genie whispered, then took Tamara by the arm and guided her to the cave's mouth. Standing behind her, he wrapped his arms about her, and together, from their hilly vantage point, they looked out over the entire palace complex.

"We're out," she sighed in relief.

"Yes, Tamara." He squeezed her close. "We're free."

Cursed

he witch-queen smiled, feeling that soft supple body nuzzled close against hers. Dawn's fingers were only just creeping though the window when she opened her eyes. Having turned slowly, so as not to waken her love, she kissed the soft red lips. She brushed the loose strands of dark hair from those full fleshy cheeks, then kissed the pale white eyelids, before slipping soundlessly from the immense, plush canopy bed. The thin silk sheet slid from her lover, and as the queen stood naked in the early preternatural light, her eyes were drawn to that peacefully sleeping form.

The pale beauty had now become a woman. For four years they had shared a bed, and the witch-queen had watched the transformation with amazement. Small, firm breasts had blossomed and taken shape, and so very sensitive were they under the queen's gentle kisses. Her body, still soft and satiny smooth to the loving caress, had lost much of its childish pudge, for the firmness of youth. With thighs of velvet below a narrow strip of thick dark curls, the queen was intoxicated with her lover's natural perfume, with the sound of soft moaning. The feel of the girl's slow sensual squirming at the queen's touch and kisses showed her beloved the ecstasy of climax.

Her eyes twinkling lovingly, the queen smiled, then turned and walked across the room. The ritual hadn't changed over seventy-five years, though she appeared to be no older than her mid-twenties. From the great oak cabinet, she drew her candles and incense, placing them

33

quickly but deliberately, with practiced skill, on the floor around her. As she knelt in the center, the candles and incense flared to light with a mere thought, and as if of their own accord, the arcane words of power flowed from her lips. The glamour spell was a familiar sensation, a warmth between her legs that, as the chant continued, flowed out, spreading to encompass her whole body, her whole being. The feeling built and built, much like sexual intimacy with her young lover, but never granted her the climactic release. As always, it took her to that edge, right to the verge of release and held her there for what felt like an eternity, before vanishing altogether, leaving her soaked in sweat, barely able to draw breath.

Finally, when she could manage some semblance of composure, the queen stood and replaced the candles and incense in the oak cabinet. She wanted to do as she had done so many times before, after the spell, wanted to climb back into bed and wake the girl, to feel the gentle touch of those alabaster hands, the soft kisses of those perfect red lips, as her beloved finished what the spell had so cruelly stopped.

Instead, however, as she had done countless times in her long life, the witch-queen removed the silk sheet, unveiling her magic mirror. Standing before it, she gathered her courage to ask the all-important question: "Mirror, mirror on the wall, who's the fairest of us all?"

It was not vanity that drove her to ask such a question, but love. She had been ten when the old witch had killed her family. The old crone had been caught, but before being put to death, she had uttered a curse, a curse that the young princess had heard and had now spent her whole life trying to reverse. The curse would bring tragedy to the fairest of them all, so since her coronation three days after her family's massacre, she had lived in, and ruled from, seclusion, studying the mystical tomes of the old witch and daily struggling against the curse that would destroy her.

The witch-queen's regularly, selflessly cast glamour spells kept the curse focused on her, ensuring the safety of her land and those she ruled. Hers was a hard and lonely life. Her people never saw her; they feared her and believed the worst: that she was hideously deformed and evil, but none dared to challenge her power. Though she ruled from seclusion, in her realm, her rule was law.

For fear of the curse, she could have no companions in her solitude, and for many long years, her heart ached. Finally, the gods took pity on her, rewarding her for the lifetime she had sacrificed for her land and people. One winter evening, as the queen sat by her open window, doing needlework and feeling the great weight of her loneliness, she accidentally pricked her finger. Jerking her hand away, a single drop of blood flew out to fall on the snow. Looking at the drop of deep red, a gentle voice whispered in her mind: "Unto you a companion is given with skin as white as snow, lips as red as blood, and hair as dark as night. You need never fear her."

In the morning, when the queen awoke and gazed out the window at her garden, she saw a figure lying outside the window. There, sleeping comfortably on a bed of soft fluffy snow, lay a pale beauty with lips as blood, and hair as night. As the queen approached, the girl's eye's fluttered open, eyes of pure innocence. The girl smiled. Though she appeared untouched by the winter's chill, the queen lifted the girl into her arms and carried her inside to warm beside the fire. Brushing the silky black curls from the girl's face, the queen smiled and said, "I will call you Snow White."

The girl only smiled and nuzzled her face into the queen's warm breast.

The next four years were the happiest of the queen's life. She still studied the ancient tomes and searched for a cure for the old witch's curse, but always made time for Snow White, and their love grew and developed. Snow White was the queen's friend, her lover, and her inspiration.

Yesterday, after seventy-five years of glamour spells, protection spells, and endless study, the witch-queen had made a breakthrough. Finally, she had found the key. The curse's end was in sight; she simply needed time to decipher the old witch's curse, and with her new knowledge, reverse it piece by piece. Just a little longer.

Beautifully regal, the queen now asked, "Magic mirror on the wall, who is the fairest of us all?"

"Snow White," the mirror replied.

"What?" she asked, stunned.

"Snow White," the mirror repeated. "Across the kingdom's breadth and height, there is none fairer than Snow White."

The queen's eyes went wide with horror as she spun on her heels to look upon the pure beauty of her young lover. "No!"

Snow White's eyes fluttered open, and she propped herself up on an elbow, a wide smile on her lips.

"No! Not her," the queen cried, spinning back to the mirror. "Anyone but her."

The smile faded from Snow White's face, replaced by a look of fear as she sat up and placed one foot on the floor, on the plush, rich carpet the queen had bought for her. "My Queen?"

Biting her lip, the witch-queen fought back the tears that threatened to overwhelm her. She turned back to the girl and forced a smile.

"What's wrong, my queen?" Snow White had never seen the queen so vulnerable; she was always so strong, so sure. The girl was afraid.

The witch-queen hurried to her side. "Nothing, my love," she lied, wrapping her arms around the girl and pulling her to her breast. "Nothing's wrong." She felt Snow White's delicate arms around her, the warmth of the girl's body pressed against her own.

"Can I help?" Snow White asked, turning her face to the queen.

Easing her embrace, the queen looked down through the mask of her own hair, into those loving eyes. Brushing her own golden locks from the child's face, the queen smiled and kissed those soft rosy lips. "Yes, actually, you can," she said, as a plan began forming in her mind.

Eyes full of adoration and expectation, Snow White waited.

Though she fought it, a tear escaped and trickled down the queen's cheek, but she held her smile, trying to ease the concern etched on her young lover's face. "You must go on a journey for me."

"A journey? Where shall I go?" she asked, her voice tinged with fear.

Having studied her whole life to protect herself, the queen knew she was unprepared and unable to protect another. But there was one place that Snow White might be safe, one place with power to rival her own.

"I need you to deliver a message for me," the Queen said, standing and gently pulling the girl to her feet. "I dare trust no one else."

Snow White could only nod. Of course, she would do anything asked of her, but she was frightened. Her queen had never before acted like this.

The queen ran to the door, locked from the inside, and opened the slot. "Summon the Huntsman."

"Yes, Your Majesty." Footfalls ran from the door as the queen slammed the slot closed. The queen hurried to her writing desk and quickly unstopped the inkwell. After a calming breath, she dipped her quill and deliberately dabbed it on the rim of the pot before putting it to the parchment and drawing large clear letters in her elegant script:

Despite my best efforts, the curse has passed to the young and precious Snow White. I have found the answer, but need time. Protect this child at all cost, with your very lives. She is innocent of mind. Protect her also from knowledge of the curse. We cannot allow it to pass again, and this child is my dearest love..

Desperately Yours,
The Queen

Her hand was shaking as she lifted it from the parchment and almost missed the quill holder. As she gently blew on the ink to speed the drying, she felt Snow White's arms around her.

"It'll be okay," the girl whispered, pressing herself close and kissing the queen's shoulder.

Standing, she turned and smiled at the innocent girl. "Yes, it *will* be okay. I will make everything okay."

Leaning up on her tiptoes, Snow White kissed the queen. "I know you will."

The queen smiled, then nodded sharply and pulled her gently to the closet. She chose her favorite dress, a velvet skirt with a blue bodice and puffy sleeves. Another tear escaped as she dressed her young lover herself, then tied on the slippers, and placed her own favorite cloak about the girl's shoulders.

A knock sounded at the door. "Your Majesty, you summoned me?"

"A moment, Huntsman," she called, loudly enough to be heard, then folded the parchment and sealed it with wax and the royal seal, before giving it to Snow White. "Stop for nothing and trust no one," the queen instructed. "I'm sending you to stay with a coven of great wizards. Remain with them and do as they instruct until I come for you. I *will* come for you."

Snow White was frightened, but nodded her understanding. "Yes, my queen."

The queen couldn't hold back the tears any longer, and they flowed freely as she kissed the child and hurried her to the door. "Huntsman."

"Your Majesty?"

"My valiant Knight, I trust you above all others."

"Thank you, Your Majesty," the Huntsman bowed deeply.

"Prove that trust is well placed. I am giving this girl into your charge. You will protect her at all cost. You will lay down your own life in defense of hers."

"Yes, Your Majesty."

"You will escort her to the dwarven keep and give her safely into their care."

"It will be done as Your Majesty commands," the Huntsman replied, looking at the girl and starting down the corridor.

"With your life, Huntsman."

"With my life," he repeated, stepping quickly.

Snow White was being hurried down the corridor. Terrified, she turned to see the queen staring after her.

"I'll come for you, my love."

Then the queen was out of sight, and Snow White was almost running to keep up with the Huntsman's quick pace.

Snow White had never traveled anywhere. The idea of leaving the castle and its surrounding hamlet both terrified and excited her. Something was wrong, and she knew it, but she didn't know what it was. The most powerful woman in the land was afraid, and that frightened her, but the queen had given her an important message to deliver. The queen had trusted her, and the girl swore she would not fail.

The morning had been chilly, and the queen's fur-lined cloak was wrapped close about as she hurried to keep pace with the tall, broad Huntsman. She fingered the sealed parchment tucked in her cloak pocket. The queen hadn't told her what it said, only that it had to be delivered. Fanciful imaginings danced through her mind. Maybe it was a magic spell to save the kingdom from a dragon, or maybe it was a message that could somehow avert certain destruction or save a lot of lives. Snow White didn't know, but guessing kept her mind off the fact that whatever was happening had the powerful witch-queen so fearful she was shaking.

The Huntsman had slowed, yet Snow White was still having a hard time keeping up. She stumbled, and he caught her.

"I'm sorry," she said, knowing she was slowing him down.

For the first time, the Huntsman, whose eyes never stopped scanning the surrounding woods, looked at her. His eyes were deep dark pools; his face was tanned and creased from a long hard life as his queen's champion. After a quick glance at the sky to see where the sun stood, he smiled. It looked unnatural on his face.

"We'll rest for a moment," he said, his strong gnarled hand guiding her to a fallen tree on which she could sit.

As she sat, Snow White untied her slippers and rubbed her sore feet. She had spent all day on her feet before and had gotten a blister, but this was going to be worse, she was certain. This was hard walking over rough terrain.

The break wasn't long, and the Huntsman never sat down. Occasionally he glanced curiously at her, but mostly he scanned the woods. After only a few minutes, he spoke without looking at her. "We should keep moving."

Nodding, Snow White retied her slippers and resumed her journey at the Huntsman's side. The Huntsman didn't speak much, and he was such a big, intimidating man that she didn't dare try to talk to him. Instead, she did her best to do as he did and watch the forest. She didn't know what to look for, but watched anyway. At first, she imagined things. A great monstrous dragon charging out of the woods to devour her, and this old warrior beside her fighting it off, or maybe it wasn't a dragon, but a band of orcs or a lion.

But as the morning progressed, and the sun neared its zenith, the day was too beautiful for such frightening beasts, and though she was still trying to keep up with the powerful Huntsman, her eyes were no longer watching for some unknown threat. Instead, Snow White was watching the leaves dance in the breeze, the birds and butterflies flutter to and fro. Squirrels and other woodland creatures skittered across the ground and through the limbs of the trees. It was all too beautiful, too wondrous to be threatening.

The Huntsman was watching her more, she noticed, watching her smile in awe at nature's splendor, watching her smell the flowers she had picked and put in her hair, watching her laugh as chipmunks chased one another. Wistful amusement played at his eyes as he watched her youthful antics, and she smiled at him.

When the sun was high in the sky, her feet ached, and her stomach rumbled so loud the Huntsman heard it. He glanced at her with upraised eyebrows, then smiled. The smile was genuine, but still didn't fit his age-scarred face.

"Let's take another break," he said, and patiently watched her sit on a stone. The Huntsman drew some jerky from his pouch and tore off a chunk with his teeth, then, almost as an afterthought, withdrew another large piece and gave it to her. "It's not much, my lady, but it will give you strength."

"Thank you," she said, taking the offered food. It was hard to bite into and tough to chew, but Snow White smiled at him as she nibbled. "It's beautiful out here," she said nervously, seeing him stare at her.

It took a moment for her words to register, and he nodded, turning again to look into the trees. Ripping off another small bite of jerky, Snow White untied her slippers again and gasped in pain as she took them off. The blisters were red and raw. In spite of the pain, she refused to cry, but rubbed her sore feet. "How far are we going?"

A long way yet, my lady," the Huntsman replied, glancing at her sore feet. "We should get there by evening, if we keep moving."

Snow White groaned, slipping her feet back into the slippers and tying them tightly.

As they resumed their journey, she tried talking to the Huntsman, who seemed to watch her more and more, but his words were few, so she gave up and walked on, whistling or humming a merry little melody. The sun had become hot, and the cloak was too much. She unclasped the chain and folded the cloak neatly over her arm, careful to keep the all-important message tucked safely away.

She tried to keep up, she really did, but as the afternoon wore on, it became so hard. The Huntsman moved so fast, and the blisters on her feet hurt so badly. She stumbled and fell, screaming as she banged her knee on a rock and skinned the palm of her hand. The Huntsman offered her his hand to help her up.

"Thank you," she said, after he had pulled her to her feet. Still feeling his hand on hers, she glanced up at him. A cloud seemed to swirl in his eyes; startled, she took an unconscious step back, away from him.

As she did, her hand slipped from his. He blinked, then shook his head, and after a moment, offered her a weak smile. "We should keep moving."

Snow White hesitated, what had just happened? As he began walking, she closed her eyes and chuckled, dismissing it as her imagination. After all, this was the Huntsman, the queen's loyal champion. "How much farther?" she asked plodding along behind him, now with a walking stick.

"We'll stay on this cart road straight to the gate," he said, glancing at the late afternoon sun, then back to her. "But it'll be getting dark by the time we get there."

Snow White groaned but pressed on, even trying to speed up the pace. Blood and dirt soaked her once white slippers. She had fallen a few more times, her knees were scraped and bruised, and the palms of her hands had been torn from landing hard on rocks and sticks. So close to her queen, she had enjoyed a pampered life until now, but her devotion to her queen was strong; she would deliver this all-important message no matter how hard it got.

The Huntsman occasionally glanced at the surrounding forest, but now he spent most of his time watching her, a strange little smile always on his face, and he walked beside her, always at the ready to catch her if she fell.

The sun was nearing the treetops in the western sky, as Snow White stumbled once more. The Huntsman caught her easily and guided her to a large stone, where he gently sat her down.

Her blistered feet were agony, and she had to work hard to fight back the tears that threatened to overwhelm her. This had all been so much, had all happened so fast. One minute she was in a warm comfy bed with the queen, and then, all of a sudden, she was on a painful march across the kingdom. Snow White was afraid, in pain, and exhausted.

"We'll camp here," the Huntsman said, watching her.

"For a couple minutes, but we can't stop."

"For the night."

"We can't," she protested. "My queen told me to stop for nothing."

Kneeling beside her, the Huntsman smiled. "Her Majesty did not mean for my lady to fall down a cliff in the dark and break her neck. It'll be dark in an hour or so."

Before she could respond, he said, "We'll camp here tonight and be at the dwarven keep in the morning."

His smile was creepy, and there was something about the way he watched her and was always so close. No, she told herself, he's close so I don't fall. He's my queen's man. She didn't want to spend the night here, but maybe he was right.

She started to get up to help, but the Huntsman told her to sit and rest, so Snow White untied and removed the slippers from her raw and blistered feet. She rested while he gathered wood and built a camp, then got some water from a stream in his hat and knelt before her.

As the sun set, spewing its myriad hues of blue, purple, and red across the horizon, the Huntsman began wiping the blood from her feet with a rag torn from her shirt. He offered what was meant to be a comforting smile as he gently dabbed around the blisters and washed her feet.

"Thank you." She smiled uneasily.

The Huntsman rose and, from a satchel on his belt, drew a small jar. After removing the stopper and lightly dipping his finger, he began dabbing the ointment onto her blisters.

"What is it?" Snow White asked.

"Magic salve to speed the healing." He never looked up. "Your feet will feel much better by morning."

It tingled and cooled the burning. Snow White leaned back on her arms as he applied it. When she thought he was done and was about to thank him, she felt him lift the hem of her dress.

"What are ... " she began, but, frightened, stopped.

"My lady's knees are badly scraped," he said offering her another creepy smile.

Stock still, Snow White watched him slide the hem of her dress up to her mid-thigh. As he used his cloth to wash her knees, his fingers seemed to linger, and she swore he was staring under her skirt, up between her legs. Her chest tightened, and she squeezed her legs closed, catching his hand between her knees. Pulling his hand free, anger flashed in his eyes, then vanished. "The salve will heal your wounds by morning."

Eyes wide, frightened, Snow White shook her head.

A flash of anger again showed again, then was gone. The Huntsman dipped his finger in the salve again and dabbed the cuts on the front of her knees, then wedged his hand between her shins. "Open up, the salve will help."

A tear tricked down her cheek, as she shook her head and tried to pull away, whimpering,

"Nooo... "

Anger flashed again. "Yes!" He jammed his hand up between her knees and forced them apart.

"No!" she screamed and hit his head, but he only leered at her as his hand slid up between her thighs. She screamed again and kicked him, but the big, burly Huntsman only laughed, catching her ankle and driving her backwards, off the stone to lie flat on her back on the hard, rocky ground.

"Stop!" She flailed and thrashed, but all in vain. He was more than a match for her. Through her tears, she saw him grinning, laughing at her as her skirt was thrown up.

"There it is," he said, his tough, leathery hand groping her.

Refusing to give up the futile fight, she kicked and flailed, screaming, begging him to stop. Her eyes went wide, and she shrieked as his finger entered her. He laughed. As her finger found his eye, his laughter turned to growling and, in one fluid movement, he withdrew his finger and slapped her hard across the face.

He was on top of her then, straddling her, her body pinned under his weight, her wrists held fast in one monstrous hand's iron grasp. She cried and squirmed as, with his free hand, he unfastened his own pants and worked them down.

Screaming and thrashing with renewed vigor, terrified, she yanked her hands free, kicking, punching, and clawing at the Huntsman. He growled and punched her. With the blow, stars danced before her eyes, dazing her, and immediately her hands were pinned again.

Through her tears, she saw him grinning wickedly, felt his hard rough kisses; his tongue licked her face, and she screamed. Unable to free her hands, she shook her head, throwing it back and forth. His face was there right beside hers, and she did the only thing she could do, she bit him. Latching hold of the flesh of his cheek, she locked her jaw as tightly as she could.

His howl of pain filled her ears. Blood from his torn face poured over her, and his hands shot to this wound. Snow White's hands were free. Her teeth still clenched tight around the chunk of meat, she jammed her thumb into his dark, swirling eye socket. He was screaming now, as she buried her thumb past the knuckle. Adrenaline surged though her veins, she heaved with all her might, throwing the Huntsman off her. Squirming and wriggling, she worked herself free and skittered back away from him.

The Huntsman's hand shot out with lightning speed and latched onto her ankle. Snow White screamed and drove her free heel into his face. His oft-broken nose collapsed under the blow. Blood gushed down his face. His ruined face, torn and bloody, contorted in rage. He lost his grip on her ankle just as her second kick landed, driving hard into his torn cheek.

Terror and adrenaline drove her as she jumped to her feet. Forgetting the blisters, forgetting all but her desperate need, Snow White grabbed the cloak with the all-important message, and ran as fast as her legs would carry her. She knew the Huntsman was up now, but she dared not turn to look. She heard him pursuing her, growling in rage. Tears poured down her face. Her vision blurred. Adrenaline surged. Snow White ran. The Huntsman chased her. She screamed.

She saw a light. Down the road was a light. A lantern burned. She ran. He was behind her. He growled. He was closing. She screamed. She ran.

A door swung open, and a small figure appeared. Blue light flashed by her, and the Huntsman howled in pain. Snow White ran toward the door as more and more blue bolts zipped past her. As she dashed inside, though the open portal, the door slammed shut.

Curling up into a little ball, and clutching her queen's cloak tight to her chest, Snow White peered around her at the five small, half-sized men who now surrounded her.

"Is she all right?" a gruff voice asked from the right.

There was a face in front of hers, with huge ears, rosy cheeks, and a bulbous nose over a big silly grin. The funny face bobbed up and down.

"Well, get out of the way, Nitwit!"

The funny face nodded, but didn't move, just grinned at her until it was roughly shoved aside, and a severe, bearded face shoved its way in. "She looks okay."

"Well, give the poor girl some room," another voice said, and the two standing over her were seemingly dragged away. "Well, hello, dear." This one was a little smaller than the first. He had kindly, grey eyes behind small square glasses and a long grey beard. He smiled warmly. "Well, well, aren't you just the prettiest little thing."

"Little?" the gruff voice asked. "Barely half grown and already bigger than you."

"I think she's perdy," a fourth man admitted. The speaker was a round little man with big brown eyes. As she caught a glimpse of him, his face flushed red, and he turned away.

"Does she have a name?" the gruff voice asked.

"Well, we'll find out, but let's give the poor girl some room. Well, back up now, back up."

"Achoo! Excuse me."

Snow White lifted her head finally and looked around at the five small men who stood staring at her.

"Are ... Are you the wizards?" she asked, still scared and shaking from the excitement

Nitwit bobbed his head

"What else would we be?" the gruff one grunted.

"Well, be nice, Buster," said the grey bearded one. "Yes, we are, Dear. Yes, we are."

"I have something from my queen." Snow White fumbled in the cloak for the sealed message.

Finally finding it, she handed it to the one who had spoken last; he seemed to be in charge.

"Well, well, a message from the queen."

"What does it ... Achoo ... say, Topper?"

"Take your damn allergy medicine," Buster growled.

Easily breaking the seal with his thumb, Topper opened and scanned the message. His face seemed to lose its luster, and all the others fell silent.

"Something's wrong," Buster grunted, his bushy eyebrows drawing down into a scowl. "There's always something wrong."

Topper's smile wasn't as bright as before, but it was gentle. "Well, Snow White is going to stay with us for a while."

"Oh, that can't be good," Buster grunted.

"Where will she sleep?" a droopy-eyed man asked with a yawn. "I don't mind if she shares with me."

Nitwit shook his head, then, grinning, puffed himself up a little bigger and stretched out his arms.

"Yes, Nitwit, we know you have the biggest bed, but that's because you flop around and fall on the floor."

Nitwit frowned, looked at Snow White and shook his head. She smiled at him as she rose to her full height. Being able to see the whole room now, she realized that two more little men were standing at the windows watching the Huntsman.

"Well, we'll find her a place to sleep," Topper said. "A place of her own." He thought for a moment, then smiled broadly and glanced around at the others. "Would anyone like to volunteer his bed for the queen's lady?"

Hands immediately shot up, and voices rose as the men argued over whose bed she could have.

"Knock it off!" Buster growled, and under his glare, all fell silent.

"Well, thank you, Buster," Topper said, considering the others' hopeful expressions. "Well, I think it might be best if Snow White has Blushy's bed, and Blushy can share with Smiley."

Blushy smiled and looked at her, immediately blushing and turning away.

When no one objected, a self-satisfied smile spread on Topper's face, and he offered one sharp nod. Snow White, who had been quiet this whole time, smiled at these nice little men and leaned against the wall, closing her eyes. After such a terrifying ordeal, she now felt safe.

"Oh, she's hurt. Look at her ... Achoo ... feet."

"Will you take your damn medicine?" Buster snarled.

"Well, Dusty's right," Topper said.

Instantly Snow White was surrounded by what felt like a hundred little men, as they bustled around, stumbling over one another. A chair appeared, and she found herself sitting. A bowl of water arrived and was promptly kicked over. A dwarf went down in the puddle, followed by another and another, until the whole lot of them lay in a heap before her. She giggled.

"Get off me," Buster shouted, and gave a mighty shove, sending Nitwit into Dusty, who was gaining his feet, knocking them both to the floor. Standing, he glared at Snow White. "What are you laughing at?"

Her face screwed up as she tried in vain to hide her smile. "Nothing."

Topper rose next, and, after brushing himself off and regaining his composure, stuck two fingers in his mouth and issued a long shrill whistle. Everyone stopped and fell silent. Topper smiled proudly, then directed the dwarves to various tasks.

In no time, a tub was filled with warm water, and sheets were hung around it for privacy.

"Have you eaten yet?" Smiley asked, poking his head in as she started undressing. She squealed in surprise.

"Get out of there!" Buster growled, jerking Smiley back roughly. "Now stay out!"

"Well, you can bathe now, Dear. No one will go in."

Snow White couldn't help smiling. She shook her head and peeled the now soiled dress up over her head. "Thank you."

"She's probably hungry," Smiley said quietly.

"Well, are you hungry, Dear?" Topper asked through the curtain.

She nodded. "Yes, very hungry." The sound of the dwarves bustling around outside the curtain made her smile. Sitting back, she closed her eyes, dipped a cloth in the warm water, and began to bathe. It felt good, like washing away all the dirt and blood somehow washed away what had happened, washed away all the fear and pain. Never having been so scared in her life; she knew beyond any doubt that the Huntsman would have killed her. How could that happen?

With all these thoughts plaguing her mind, her bath wasn't as relaxing as it had been. Quickly finishing, she was about to put her torn and soiled dress back on, when a voice sounded just outside the curtain.

"I'm sure it's not as nice as you're accustomed to, my lady, but we found some clothes for you to wear when you're done."

"Thank you, Smiley," she said, seeing his silhouette through the curtain. "Can you pass them under?"

He bobbed his head and lifted the curtain just enough to slide the small bundle of clothes underneath.

"Thank you," she said as he scampered off.

The clothes appeared to be one of the dwarves' nightshirts and a bed sheet.

Snow White smiled. She pulled the night shirt over her head and found that it was big and puffy on her, but only came down to her mid-thighs. Then she folded the sheet in half and tied two corners on her left hip. Her new skirt was open along one leg, but, she decided, would do just fine.

After washing her dress as well as she could and hanging it up to dry, Snow White went to dump the water basin out the window. A feeling of unease crept over her. Looking up, she found its source. There, by the tree line stood the Huntsman, or what had been the Huntsman. His eyes glowed, and he stared at her unblinking. His shoulders were hunched and he looked little like the queen's champion with whom she had set out that morning.

"You're safe here," Buster said from beside her. She hadn't heard him come up, but now he stepped closer and looked out the window with her. "It can't get to you now."

"He was supposed to protect me," Snow White whispered.

"I know, and I'm sure he did for as long as he could, but he wasn't prepared for an enemy such as this."

"What do you mean?"

"Come away from the window, Dear," Topper instructed, taking her by the hand and guiding her to the table. "You're safe here, so eat up."

Famished, Snow White allowed herself to be seated as a thick porridge was poured into her bowl.

Picking up her spoon, she looked around. They were all watching her. "Aren't you going to eat too?"

They looked at one another, then scrambled to seat themselves and began filling their own bowls. Now she noticed for the first time that they were all wearing amulets around their necks, amulets they had not been wearing when she arrived. She was about to ask when Topper spoke.

"We don't have any private rooms, but while you bathed, we surrounded your bed with sheets to give you some privacy."

"Thank you." She smiled at these men who were being so kind to her.

After they had eaten, Snow White was shown to her bed. It wasn't as long as she was tall, but it looked very comfy, especially after the day she'd had.

She offered her thanks and lay down, certain she'd be asleep in seconds. Sleep, however, eluded her. Instead she tossed and turned, replaying over and over the day's events. Hours later she realized that the dwarves had not gone to bed. Thirsty and unable to sleep, Snow White slipped from her bed and crept from the large bed chamber.

"Man the north wall; don't let it in," someone yelled.

A wave of fear washed over her at the thought of the Huntsman. Part of her said to run back to bed and hide, but another wanted to know what was going on. Her attention was drawn to the windows as a blue ball went streaking past.

Running over to look outside, she arrived in time to see the Huntsman, now a hideously deformed monster, get hit by a large barrage of small blue balls. The monster screamed, an unnatural sound that filled the night.

"Careful now, don't kill it," Buster hollered, "If its host dies, it'll take another form."

"Yes," another agreed, "and we don't know what that form might be. Defend against it, but for the dear girl's sake, don't kill it,"

"Not just the girl's sake," someone corrected, "the kingdom's."

Terrified, unable to move, Snow White watched as the monster threw itself time and again at the wall right in front of her window, never taking its eyes off her: its red, glowing eyes. Blue ball after blue ball hit the monster, but with inhuman endurance, it stubbornly struggled on.

"What is it doing?" a dwarf yelled.

"Shut up and fight," another screamed. "Don't let it in!"

Snow White's eyes were the size of saucers. She stared at the ghastly beast bearing down on her.

One foot behind the other, she finally backed away as tears blurred her vision. Dwarven shouts filled the air, and under their assault, the approaching monster became only a blurry blue glow.

Finally, the monster stopped. In the midst of the magical bombardment, it became still. Its eyes never left her as it lifted its arm and pointed at her. Opening its mouth, it emitted such a high-pitched and unnatural scream that the dwarf magicians' yelling was drowned out completely.

Snow White's hands shot up to her ears, but they were scant protection from the pain of that piercing shriek. It seemed to go on forever. Snow White began to weep and fell to her knees. As she watched, a massive blue orb, sizzling with energy, blasted the creature, hurling it backward to land at the base of an apple tree, where it was finally, mercifully silent.

A ringing filled Snow White's head. She didn't hear anyone approach, but almost immediately she found she was surrounded by her new dwarf protectors. Buster looked mad as he seemed to be yelling at her, but others smiled comfortingly or just looked relieved that she was okay. Topper's gentle hand helped her up and started guiding her back to the bedroom. Wanting to be certain that she really was safe, Snow White turned to look out the window one last time.

She stopped and stared. Even as she watched, the accursed monster melted and vanished into the ground, until nothing remained but the Huntsman's torn and battered clothes. He was gone.

Snow White didn't remember going to bed, but awoke with the mid-morning sun streaming through the window. Moving the curtain, she sat up on the edge of the small bed and gave a mighty yawn, stretching her arms as far as they would go.

"You're awake," Smiley yelled excitedly. "She's awake!"

Smiling at the grey-bearded, balding man, Snow White stood and snugged up the knot at her hip that had loosened as she slept, then turned and made the bed.

"Are you hungry, my lady," Smiley asked, as he pulled the blanket tight on the other side. "I bet some eggs and fruit would fix you right up."

"Thank you." She smiled at him, then realized just how hungry she was. Breakfast sounded nice.

Last night's events flooded her mind, and she stood still, "That thing."

"Don't worry. You're safe here, my lady. The monster is gone." Smiley took her hand and pulled her gently toward the kitchen. "You'll feel better once you eat."

"But last night," she began, remembering all she had heard. "Someone said it would take another form."

Smiley nodded slowly, then looked up and his face lit. "But you're safe here. These amulets," he held up the amulet that she had noticed the day before. "They protect us from the curse. It can't touch us. And the keep is warded for protection. You're safe here."

Comforted by his confidence, Snow White ate breakfast and tried to relax. "Where are the others?" Only Smiley and Blushy were there with her.

"They're working. We mine ore and then use our skills in alchemy to turn it into gold."

"You make gold?"

Blushy smiled and turned away, but Smiley nodded. "Sort of. We use our talents to alter its properties, to change it on a base level into gold. We need the right ores to have the proper base make-ups, then we rearrange them. It's kind of a mix and match to turn a small amount into gold, and the rest into solid stones for building. We don't really make gold; we just rearrange the compounds to ... It's complicated. "

Over the next few days, Snow White asked others about what they did. Some, like Buster, just said it was secret, but others tried to tell her. She listened carefully, but none of the others could explain it any better than Smiley had.

Although she was a guest, Snow White did all she could to help out. She cleaned the keep, washed their clothes, and cooked the meals. She was grateful for their help and kindness, so always kept a smile on her face, but inside she longed for the queen, longed to look into her eyes, feel her loving touch, and listen to that voice that had comforted her for so long, that had whispered words of love as she drifted off to sleep. Hidden behind the curtains of her bed, Snow White cried herself to sleep, wanting only to be reunited with her queen.

Every morning, when the dwarven alchemists set out for work, two remained at the keep to keep an eye on Snow White, to ensure that the dead witch's curse found no way to harm the innocent beauty. While they kept her company, she set to work and quickly developed a routine to complete her chores, then sat before a window gazing out at the warm autumn day.

Back at the castle, the queen had an impenetrable private garden where she and Snow White had spent so much time together. After making love on the plush carpet of grass, exhausted and soaked in sweat, Snow White would prop herself on an elbow and smile as the queen stood and walked to the flower beds. The queen would snap a stem, then wink before enveloping the newly broken stem of the plant, and there, before Snow White's eyes, the plant would grow to a new bud that in a day or two would open into a new beautiful flower. No matter how many times she saw the queen do this, it always amazed and delighted her. The queen would come back, a mischievous twinkle in her eye, lie down beside her, and give her the newly plucked flower. "A treasure," she would say, "for my most beloved treasure." Accepting the token of adoration, Snow White would kiss the queen's full red lips and curl up close as the queen's soft caresses glided over her body.

Now, looking out at the bright autumn days, Snow White sorely missed her queen. She had asked her guardians before to let her go outside, but none would allow it. They said it was just too dangerous. On the fifth day, however, it was Nitwit and Blushy who had stayed to protect her, and these two of all doted on her.

"Nitwit," she said, stepping close and ruffling his hair, which promptly fell over his eyes. "I want to go outside."

He shook his head adamantly, then peered up at her through his unmanageable curls.

"You two would be with me, and we'd stay close to the keep. I'm sure that you, Nitwit, would be more than enough to protect me, but with both of you ... " She smiled at Blushy. "Nothing could hurt me."

Again, Nitwit shook his head, but with clearly less resolve.

Snow White put on her best pouting face and brushed the hair from Nitwit's eyes. "Just for a few minutes. I can't stand being cooped up in here." She looked pleadingly at him. "I need to feel the sun on my face. Look out there," she said, pointing out the window. "What danger could lurk on such a beautiful day?"

Nitwit twitched his mouth back and forth, looking at her, then Blushy, then out the window, before turning back to her.

"Pleeaasse?"

He slouched, obviously defeated, and held up his fingers about an inch apart.

"Oh yes," Snow White readily agreed. "Only for a very short time. A few minutes will be enough. I just have to get outdoors."

Blushy looked uncertain, but followed Nitwit's lead as he led the way to the door, unbarred it, and opened it just a crack. A little wider, and a little wider, until he could poke his head out and peek around. After looking one way and then the other, then all around, he squeezed his way out though the door, holding up his hand for them to stay. On tip-toes he slinked to the right, then quickly to the left, before turning and nodding for them to follow.

As soon as she stepped out, Snow White felt the sun's warmth on her face. She laughed and twirled around in circles on the grass. Running to a wild lilac bush, she plucked two flowers, wishing that she could do as the queen did and make them grow back. Her frown couldn't last though, not on such a wonderful day. With a bright smile on her face, she danced back to where Nitwit and Blushy stood, both watching her and keeping an eye out for danger. She kissed each of them on the cheek and gave them the flowers, then with a light heart, danced away across the grass.

As she looked around, absorbing the sun's warmth, she saw the apple orchard and got an idea. It wasn't far, so she waved for the dwarves to follow. "I want to pick some apples to make apple pie for desert tonight."

Nitwit held up his fingers again.

"I know," she nodded. "It'll only take a moment, then we'll go back inside."

When the dwarves nodded their assent, she lifted the hem of her dress for a basket and began to pluck apples from the branches. Then she saw it, so perfect it shined with the mid-day light, such a deep red and absolutely flawless. The tree looked somehow familiar as Snow White ran to it and reached for the perfect apple.

"No!" Blushy yelled, recognizing where the cursed Huntsman had melted into the ground. He ran as fast as his little legs would carry him, but as soon as she had touched the apple, she was bewitched. The dwarves could only watch as she lifted the apple to her lips and bit loudly into the crisp, fresh fruit, a sound that reverberated throughout the land.

Snow White's eyes went wide, only then recognizing the tree and realizing her doom. As the curse coursed through her veins and a dying breath escaped her lips, she saw her queen appear out of thin air and fall to her knees. Tears filled the queen's eyes, and the last thing Snow White heard was her lover's scream of anguish.

Day after day, the witch-queen had poured over her magical tomes, deciphering the curse and preparing her cure. Physically exhausted and magically drained, she struggled on, refusing to rest until she worked out every detail to reverse the old witch's curse and free both her lover and her kingdom. After every step of the process, over a dozen times a day, she approached her mirror and asked: "Mirror, mirror on the wall, who's the fairest of us all?"

The response was always the same. "Across the kingdom's breath and height, there is none fairer than Snow White." With this reassurance of her lover's safety, she resumed her work.

Finally, she had it; she was certain that every part of the curse was accounted for and reversed in her own spell. Now, after seventy-five years, she had the means to save her land. She only needed to sleep to regain the power necessary to cast so powerful a spell.

Just as she blew out a deep sigh of satisfaction, a loud crunching echo sounded though her window. The witch-queen hastily tried to identify the sound. She couldn't, but her heart sank. She intuitively knew that something was terribly wrong.

Jumping to her feet, she ran to the mirror, "Mirror, mirror on the wall, who's the fairest of us all?"

"Across the kingdom's breadth and ... You are my queen."

"No!" The witch-queen screamed in anguished rage. Potion in hand, she cast a quick traveling spell, and in the blink of an eye appeared before the dwarven keep. There before her lay her beloved Snow White, the cursed apple still in her hand. Weeping bitterly, the witch-queen fell to the ground beside Snow White and lifted her into her loving arms. Burying her face against the girl's small breast, she wept. With great heaving sobs, she screamed out her anguish, listening as the steady thump ... thump ... thump ... of the girl's heart slowed to a stop.

She had only seconds in which to act, and act she must. Pulling the wax stopper from the vial of her potion, the witch-queen began chanting and poured the cure into Snow White's mouth and onto the accursed apple. There before her eyes, the apple faded from its enticing luster to a dull ordinary fruit, but no change came over the girl. The curse was gone, but it had claimed its victim. The witch-queen's renewed cries of agony at her loss ripped through the air, echoing far and wide. Holding her beloved close, her tears poured forth. She had lived a life of solitude for so many years before being given Snow White, the love of her life. She couldn't imagine even another day without the girl's smile to brighten her day.

"Mystic Powers from the Corners Four," she intoned, "Hear my plea, I do implore. That this innocent may yet live, all my years I freely give." She felt the power flair within her, then flow out though her body into the girl's.

All had gone black; the last thing Snow White had seen was her beloved's face, but now she felt a strange warmth flowing into and through her body; air filled her lungs, and a slow but steady thumping returned to her chest. Light flooded her eyes, the light of a warm autumn day, and as her vision cleared, she saw the queen's loving eyes staring back at her.

Snow White smiled, taking in the image of her lover, but something was different. There was no doubt that it was her queen, no doubt at all, but she had changed. The flawless satiny skin had become dark and deeply lined, and her lush long blond hair was now limp and white.

"My queen?" Snow White asked.

The queen nodded. "Yes, my love."

"What ... what happened? Are you ..."

The queen smiled and kissed Snow White. "I am old. I have spent my life struggling against a dark evil, and finally, after all these years, I have won."

"But ..."

"Shh ..." the queen silenced Snow White, pressing her finger to the girl's lips. "After a lifetime of solitude, the gods blessed my life by bringing you into it, and now in this new age of peace, this land needs a new queen. Free from evil curses and ancient ways, you will rule with wisdom and love.

"No," Snow White cried, sitting up. "You are the queen. You can't ..."

"Hush," the queen said, smiling. "I have freed you and this land I love from the grip of that ancient evil. My part has been played. But you, my young queen, free from ancient horrors, will bring this kingdom into a new era."

"No. I can't be queen," Snow White cried as tears blurred her vision.

"You ..." the queen coughed and fell into Snow White's arms. "You will be a good queen."

"But ..."

"Listen to me." When Snow White nodded silently, the queen spoke softly. "I'm dying. Nothing can stop that now. But I'm at peace. You have been the most precious thing in my life, and you are queen now."

"I'll try." Snow White wept, burying her face against her queen's breast.

"You'll be a good queen," the dying queen whispered as she struggled to draw breath. "Always let love guide you, and you'll be fair and just."

"I will," Snow White said, lifting her head to look at her dying love.

The old queen smiled and uttered her final words, "I know."

The dwarves helped Snow White take the old queen back to her castle. She was buried with a great ceremony, and, as the new queen, Snow White declared the day that the curse was banished as a holiday in honor of the old queen.

As her beloved had instructed, her rule was guided by love, and she reigned over a time of great peace and prosperity.

The Pink Rose

"**S**he's beautiful," Thor exclaimed from the window overlooking the courtyard as he gazed upon his bride-to-be for the first time. Her small stature and slight build were obvious despite the fur-lined cloak that she pulled tightly closed against the harsh winter air. Her long hair was the color of the summer sun and framed a soft, gentle face with bright blue eyes, so wide and full of wonder, taking in the magnificent castle and crowds that surrounded her.

"Finally," his mother sighed as she walked into the sitting room where the priestess and her charge would arrive presently. In keeping with tradition, her straight black mourning dress had been replaced by a full-skirted yellow taffeta gown embroidered around the hem, collar, and sleeves with tiny colorful flowers. A small bejeweled crown graced her elaborately braided honey-brown locks—now sparingly streaked with grey. Despite the weight of years on the throne and her own recent tragedy, her soft blue eyes still shone with the gaiety of the day, for this was the day of her son's nuptials.

Prince Thor was tall and strong, his muscles honed by countless hours of training with the kingdom's greatest swordsmen. He wore his topknot braided over neat shoulder-length hair, and his upper lip bore the beginnings of a mustache he hoped would become as thick as his father's. Soft brown eyes and a slightly crooked nose reflected the duality of his character: kindness and concern for his fellow man and a willingness, even eagerness, to fight for what he thought was right.

No one had expected this wedding to come for many more years. But it had, and too soon. Not choice, but necessity drove them forward now.

Thor scratched the itchy new flesh that covered his knuckles from the bar brawl he had caused on that fateful night, the night his life had been shattered.

"Thor."

Something in the sound of his mother's voice had stopped him in his tracks, and he had turned to peer into her sitting room. She was slumped in an ornately carved mahogany chair, her hands wringing a white handkerchief. Tears streaked her pale face as she had stared at him, broken by grief.

Hurrying over and kneeling before the queen, he had asked, "Mother, what is it?"

"The king, your father ..." she had choked. "He's dead."

He had held her hand as her explanation had quickly deteriorated into heaving sobs, and she had collapsed to the floor where they shared an embrace of grief and tears, had shared the weight of their mutual loss.

Time had been indeterminable. It passed without notice, but, eventually, his mother returned to her chair. Tears wiped and the wrinkles smoothed from her gown, her regal bearing had been restored, and she was again every bit the queen. Her next words had sounded stiff as if she were passing sentence on a condemned man.

"Your life is no longer your own, Thor. Your decisions no longer serve just you. They serve your people."

"I don't think I can be king," he had confessed around the lump in his throat. "I'm nothing like Father. I'm not ready."

Her eyes had softened. "No one is ever ready for the burden of duty, but your father was a fine example, and he did his best to prepare you."

Thor could only nod, trying unsuccessfully to swallow the lump in his throat.

Her voice had hardened. "Before he went off to battle, the king and I arranged a marriage for you. A messenger has already been dispatched to Freja's temple, requesting that the High Priestess Olga deliver her charge to the castle post haste."

"Marriage?" His stomach had twisted at the word, and the persistent lump threatened to suffocate him.

"Halya Olofsdottir is the orphaned daughter of a long and noble line," she explained and then smiled at him. "We haven't met her yet, but Halyas's beauty is said to rival the lights of the northern sky."

"Marriage?" he said again.

"Custom and tradition dictate that you cannot become king until you are wed."

The persistent lump refused to go away.

Now, fourteen days later, even as he mourned his father's death and struggled to be the man his people needed him to be, he waited with great anticipation to meet, for the first time, the girl who would become his wife.

Leaving the window, he walked to his mother's side, trying not to fidget, trying to act like a king. Recalling his father's stoic posture, he tried to mimic him. Thankfully, he did not have long to wait before their guests were announced to the assemblage of court officials.

"Queen Gerta and Prince Thor, may I present Olga, High Priestess and Beloved of Freja ..." The woman's entrance was brisk, moving with purpose, her whole being radiating power and authority. Resplendent in the finery of her office, she struck a majestic figure. Her austere grey dress, buttoned to her throat, did little to disguise her aged beauty. The velvet fabric barely contained her wide hips and full bosom. Long silver hair cascaded over her shoulders and extended past her thick buxom waist. But it was her eyes, her seemingly omniscient azure blue eyes, deeply set in a spider web of crows' feet, that unnerved him. Those preternatural orbs burned past his bravado and pretenses to lay his soul bare.

"... and her charge, the lovely Halya Olafsdottir." In the powerful and aged priestess' wake entered a delicate snowdrop: the girl he had observed through the window minutes before.

Both bowed deeply.

When the priestess spoke, her voice was like molasses, poignant and smooth. "Your Highness, esteemed members of the Royal Court. The king was a good and noble man. We offer our sympathy but encourage you to take heart for his was a good death. There is no doubt the Valkyries have carried him to Valhalla where he sups this very night at the Allfather's table."

"Thank you," the queen said, motioning for them to rise, then toward some empty chairs in a single sweeping gesture. "Please, sit down."

As everyone sat, refreshments were delivered by half a dozen servants. Just for something to occupy his hands, Thor wanted to eat a piece of brown bread but did not want to be the first to grab at the food. He hid his impatience as he waited for the two older women to partake.

"I received your letter," his mother began, leaving the refreshments untouched. "I understand you have some concerns you wish to address, but I believe the details were all worked out when you last met with the king."

"Arrangements were made, Your Highness, but I don't think any of us expected this union to happen quite so soon. I do, as you say, have some concerns."

Young Halya sat motionlessly; only her eyes moved as she scanned the room. It seemed to Thor that she was trying to take it all in: the cold stone walls and the warm fireplace, the simple décor of his mother's sitting room and the grand tapestries that were hung for this occasion. He wondered what it must be like to see it all for the first time. Was she simply awed by the grandeur or overwhelmed by the suffocating stateliness? Was she dreading the weight of her new status or, even now, imagining that it would all soon be hers?

He tried to catch her eyes as they roamed the room, but she never made eye contact. Instead, her gaze alighted upon the refreshments, and her full, pink lips parted to reveal a timid tongue that licked gently at their edges.

Ignoring the assortments of food arrayed around her, the queen sat quietly, her eyes locked with Olga's, wordlessly asking her to elaborate, almost demanding it.

"Your Highness, my concerns are of a delicate nature." The priestess paused significantly. "May I speak freely?"

In the queen's eyes, a thundercloud brewed, but her calm, regal bearing betrayed nothing as she dismissed the servants and the royal court.

"If I may be blunt, Your Highness," the priestess began when only the four of them remained. "I have concerns about Halyas's safety ..."

The queen's brow drew up. "Her safety?"

"Prince Thor has quite a reputation. He's known far and wide as a brawler, a gambler, and a womanizer."

Thor's face flushed at the words, feeling their sting for the first time. He scratched the new pink flesh on his knuckles as if it were the source of that sting.

"Thor was young. He was at a difficult stage of his life. He was no longer a boy but hadn't yet committed to accepting the responsibilities of manhood."

The food forgotten, Thor shuffled uneasily and tried not to fidget. Feeling her gaze, he looked at Halya, who immediately turned away in embarrassment.

"We indulged his recklessness," the queen continued, "because he was at that rebellious stage of life where he struggled against convention and experimented with life to find out who he really is."

"Therein lies my concern." Olga glared at Thor. "The boy is reckless."

Thor tried to swallow the lump that had returned to his throat. Glancing furtively at Halya, he saw that his bride-to-be's face was as red as he imagined his own was. The older women were talking about them as if they were not even there.

"The *Crown Prince*," his mother emphasized his title, "has put his selfish and childish ways behind him. He understands the responsibilities that are his birthright and his duty. Prince Thor *will* be king."

The priestess nodded. "Of course. My concern is …" She considered her words. Laying a hand on Halya's arm, she continued. "Halya deserves the same kind of *loving* and *faithful*," she offered Thor a sideways glance, "relationship that you enjoyed with the king."

"I can assure you that Thor understands that marriage is commitment and hopes to provide Halya the same kind of stable and loving home his father gave me. He is no longer a child and has, therefore put away his toys."

"I understand." The priestess' tone was conciliatory. "I have given a lifetime to the service of my goddess. Now, in the twilight of my life, Halya's well-being and happiness," she smiled lovingly at her charge, "are the most important things in the world to me."

"You have raised her into a precious young woman." The hard edge of his mother's voice had softened; the thundercloud was gone. "Now is the time to pass that torch to someone else who will love, cherish, and protect her as much as you have."

The imposing old woman turned her steely gaze on Thor. "Will you be a good husband?"

Trying to swallow the lump that refused to go away, he nodded. "I will be the best husband I can be." That was not enough, he knew. "I will try my very best to live up to the standards my father set, to make him proud, and," he offered his bride-do-be a gentle smile, "to make Halya happy.

The wedding was held on the winter solstice with extravagant celebration. It was a gala event, attended by nobles and commoners alike. With this union came a sense of hope for a new era led by a youthful king and queen. It was the dawn of a new age, and the people rejoiced. The coronation was to take place when the sun was at its apex on the day after the wedding.

On their wedding evening, with the full moon high in the sky, Halya was led off by her ladies, who would remove her grand gown and prepare her for the consummation of her marriage.

Thor was excited, and, when he received the signal that his bride was ready for him, it took all his strength to restrain himself from running. He made a stately exit and walked to his bedroom. This was special, not like all the tavern wenches and servant girls he had bedded. This was meaningful, his first night with the woman who would be his queen, would bear his children, the woman with whom he hoped to share a love as powerful as his parents' love had been.

Opening the door, he felt the excitement of unwrapping a present. He wanted to whip it open and run to her but refused to act in such a manner. Instead, he savored the moment; he opened the door slowly and closed it gently behind himself. A few lamps shed their pale-yellow light, and there she stood, angelic, in the glow of the bright full moon. A sheer white robe hung from her shoulders and gathered on the floor around her bare feet. The moon's rays passed through her robe, making it transparent and revealing every gentle curve of her body's dark silhouette. Her fingers knotted in the cloth, kneading it as she nervously chewed her full red lower lip.

"You're beautiful." He smiled, tossing his jacket aside as he slowly walked over to her. "So very beautiful."

Seeing her eyes dance nervously to him and away, Thor stepped close and brushed a few loose strands of bright yellow hair from her cheek, then gently lifted her chin to gaze into her bright blue eyes. "I won't hurt you, Halya," he said, a soft smile on his lips and in his eyes.

"I know." Her voice cracked, and she looked away.

His fingers lightly stroked her soft cheek, and when her eyes turned back up to his, he lowered his head and kissed her, letting his lips just brush hers. Thor moved slowly, gently kissing her and caressing her cheeks and neck with his fingertips. He led her the few feet to the bed and gently laid her down. Her wide eyes never left his, like a rabbit that knew it was about to die.

He didn't know what to do, didn't know how to handle this situation. He had been with many girls, but none so fragile. He wanted her to feel good, to welcome him, to kiss him. His lips found her neck, and he kissed her as he knew women liked to be kissed. Slowly, his kisses moved down over her throat and chest. Nuzzling aside the sheer robe, his lips found her small, firm breasts, and he burned with desire. Her fingers were not in his hair; no moans escaped her lips. Raising himself on his elbow, he smiled gently at his bride. That's when he saw it. Her eyes were squeezed shut, and in the corner of her right eye glistened a single tear.

"What's wrong?" he asked, confused.

"I'm sorry," she choked, then lost control and started crying. "I'm so sorry."

"Shh," he hushed, sitting up and pulling her close. "It's okay." He pulled her robe closed and kissed her forehead. "We don't have to do anything tonight. We'll take this slowly." He rocked her gently and, before long, Halya had fallen asleep against his chest.

The next morning, she apologized again, and he stroked her hair, assuring her it was okay; they would have many nights together.

They got up. There was much to do in preparation for their coronation. Halya was ushered off by her ladies, and Thor was left alone. After climbing from the bed and removing his wedding attire, he was reaching for some fresh clothes when a sound behind him drew his attention. He turned to see one of his wife's ladies-in-waiting watching him, a smile on her lips, a smile he knew well.

For a moment, they just looked at each other. Something stirred within him, and he saw the girl's eyes move down his body. His smile turned to a grin as he rose to the occasion. He crossed the distance between them in an instant and pressed his mouth needfully to hers. Feeling her hands on his shoulders and back, Thor picked her up and dropped her on the bed. He tore her dress open and kissed her full round breasts. As she moaned in pleasure, he ripped the dress to its hem and lay atop her. She grabbed him and pulled him as he positioned himself, then drove himself inside her. As she cried with pleasure, his lips found her neck. Her fingers clutched at his back; he bit her neck.

"Harder," she cried, and he obliged. He bit her neck harder and thrust himself deeply and powerfully inside her. He tasted blood but didn't stop. Her moans of desire drew him on harder and harder until, at last, he exploded inside her.

"No!"

Thor turned at the sound to see his gentle, young wife staring at him. "Halya," he started, but what could he say?

Halya burst into tears, and, to Thor's utter amazement and horror, sheran to the window, and, without a word, hurled herself through it.

Thor dashed from the bed and ran to the window. There, on the rocks below, lay the crumpled form of his beautiful new bride.

"No!"

He turned and came face to face with Olga, the high priestess who had raised Halya from childhood. She looked out the window at the twisted and broken caricature of a human body below. She rounded on him, her eyes like the very pits of hell. "You!"

"I …" he started, but she cut him off.

"You killed her!"

"No! She jumped," Thor argued, still stunned by all that had happened.

Fury burned in Olga's eyes, and Thor was forced back by the power of her rage. "You monster! You killed my little girl!"

The lady-in-waiting, deciding it was an appropriate time to leave, started slipping from the bed, but Olga spun on her. "And you!" The girl froze. Olga uttered an incantation, and the girl began to scream.

Thor could do nothing, only watch in horror as the girl's hands and feet transformed into cold, hard stone. She screamed and twisted in agony as the transformation continued inward. At last, with her mouth forever open in a soundless scream and her body contorted inhumanly, the echoes of her agony faded into silence.

As Olga turned on Thor, he lifted his hands defensively. "Please, don't kill me."

She glared at him with pure hatred. "No, my prince, I cannot kill you. By my oath, sworn so many years ago, I cannot kill the royal blood."

Thor sighed in relief and was about to apologize and explain that he had never meant her any harm, but the old priestess wasn't finished. "I can't kill you, young prince, but I can promise that you'll wish I had."

"Olga, I ..." he began, but she cut him off again.

"You, who have never known love but, instead, have killed it. You, who are a monster, no better than a primal beast, will bear witness on the outside to what you are on the inside."

As soon as she finished these words, Olga intoned an incantation, and Thor knew pain as he had never imagined. The sounds of his own bones breaking and his screams of agony filled his ears. His vision blurred and lost its color. The pain continued, and his body was broken and twisted until, mercifully, Thor lost consciousness.

When he woke again, the pain was unbearable; every inch of his body hurt. His eyes fluttered open, and there, cradling his head in her lap, was his mother. Tears poured down her cheeks as she gently touched his face. There was no color in his vision; he blinked, but it remained unchanged, just varying shades of gray.

"Mother?" His voice, now deep and guttural, sounded strange in his own ears.

"My son," she cried, her lip quivering. "I don't have much time, so listen closely. Olga has cursed you into this hideous form, but I have prayed, and the goddess Frigg has heard my pleas."

"What do you ..." Thor began, but his mother hushed him.

"I have to tell you this. It's important, so listen. Frigg has answered my prayers and has given you a way out. You must find true love, my son. You have twenty years in which to find a girl who will love you for who you are on the inside to break this outward curse. But, if you do not find love in that time, then the curse will stand, and you will be a monster forever. I know the truth of what's inside you, Thor, and Frigg has granted me this chance to prove it, to undo this evil."

"But ..."

Again, she hushed him. "Listen, Thor. Listen closely. In a moment, the goddess will transform me, my life given for you." She silenced him before he could argue. "My essence remade into a symbol of my sacrifice, I will become a flower with twenty petals, and one petal will fall away every year on the anniversary of the curse. You must find love before the last petal falls to the floor."

"No, Mother! You can't!" he cried in the deep guttural voice that was not his own.

She smiled. "It's done."

With these words, the room was filled with a blinding flash. Thor could see its vibrancy, even with his new vision. Its brilliance hung for a moment, engulfing the whole room, and then began to fade until only a rose remained. As she had foretold, his mother was transformed, and where she had been a moment ago stood a beautiful, glowing, rose. It stood on its diagonally-cut stem and slowly revolved around and around.

For some time, he could not move but lay on the floor watching the rose through tear-blurred vision. When he could finally stand, he lifted his mother's rose onto the wooden mantel over the fireplace where it continued to rotate. Turning, he saw the girl, who had been his lover, twisted inhumanly into a silent scream. He left the room, escaping its horrors, only to hear cries of terror from all who looked at him. He tried to speak to them, to explain, but everyone ran away before he could tell them what had happened.

In moments, he was face to face with his own guards. They stabbed at him with spears and slashed with mighty axes. This new body was fast and strong. Thor dodged blow after blow as he tried to explain who he was, but they didn't care. They saw only a monster. Forced to fight or die, Thor fought, and, when the battle ended, he was the undisputed lord of his castle.

During the fight, everyone else had fled while the soldiers held the monster at bay. When all were safely out of the castle, the surviving guards ran, carrying their wounded, leaving their dead.

Olga was there when Thor entered the grand hall. She smiled wickedly and turned to leave.

"I will break this curse!" he shouted at her.

"Impossible." She laughed at him.

Thor screamed at her. "My mother's death will not be in vain. I will find love, and I WILL break this curse."

She spun then, her smile gone. "Your mother's death?"

Realizing he had said more than he should have, Thor fell silent.

Olga stared at him for a moment; then her eyes went wide as if struck by a revelation. The rage he had seen before returned. "You'll never find love!" she screamed as she dashed outside. "You'll never break my curse. No one will come near this castle, or they will die trying."

With that, she melted into the ground, and, even as he watched, a great, dark woods grew up around the castle as far as the eye could see. As Thor's mother had given her life for a chance to break the curse, Olga had given hers to prevent it from being broken. All her hate was poured into these enchanted woods, making it a terrible, dangerous place. It was alive with sinkholes and murderous vines. To enter was to risk one's very life as Olga's hate and corruption compelled the woods to kill any who would dare traverse it. Only Thor's new strength, speed, and agility allowed him to hunt in and survive it.

Fifteen years passed. Fifteen years of solitude, loneliness, and despair. Thor had been hunting in the woods to survive, and it had left its marks on his now badly scarred body and on his spirit. He hadn't bothered to get dressed for years. Carcasses lay where he had eaten them. Not bothering to eat at the table or even cook his food, he sat on the floor wherever was convenient and tore his meat from the fresh kill, leaving the remains to rot and fester.

The day after the winter solstice, Thor was in his family's old living room where he had played as a boy and where he still felt close to his past. Talking to the rose that was his mother's essence, where it stood on the end table in the sun, he watched another petal break free and float slowly to the floor. This agony was more than he could bear. She had given her life so he could have a chance to break this curse, but her efforts were in vain; her death was for nothing. Enraged, Thor screamed and went into a fury, throwing and breaking anything that wasn't tied down. Lamps and chairs, tables and books; everything was smashed against the wall and destroyed.

When his anger had played itself out, he fell to his knees amid the wreckage and cried. A warm glow lit the room and comforted him. It calmed him as if his mother's arms were wrapped lovingly around him.

After he had recovered, Thor turned to smile warmly at the rose, only to find that, in his rage, it had been damaged. An inch from the bottom, its stem was broken, causing it to rotate awkwardly on its axis.

"No," he whispered, crawling over and gently lifting it. For a moment, he wept as he held it, held all that remained of his beloved mother. He was unsure what to do to fix it but knew he could not leave it like this.

"I'll take care of you," he promised, terrified of doing more damage but having to do something. From the kitchen, he retrieved a knife, so small in his huge meaty hands, and gently, deliberately, cut the stem diagonally just above the break. He held it for a moment, afraid to put it down, afraid of what might happen, but, as it glowed brightly, reassuringly, he held his breath and took a chance. Returning to the fireplace, he carefully placed the rose on the mantle. Gingerly, he released the rose and watched as it glowed brightly and, standing on its newly cut stem, began to rotate.

"Oh, thank the goddess," Thor sighed in relief, stepping back and watching his precious rose turn as it had before.

Turning and looking around, he saw the mess he had made. Overcome by shame, his eyes were drawn back to the beautiful rose in the ruined room. Knowing he couldn't leave her in here, he took the rose delicately in his giant hand and left the room. In the hall, he looked each way, uncertain where to go. There was one place, one place that he had never been able to enter in all these years. At the end of the hall was his mother's sitting room. To him, it was holy ground, but now this sacred room was the only place left that felt right to put her, to talk to her, the only place worthy of her.

Taking a deep breath and building up his courage, he took a few hesitant steps, slowly approaching that most hallowed ground. At the door, he stopped, his hand shaking as he reached for the handle. The soft glow of the rose intensified at his hesitation, comforting him as his mother had so many times before. With this reassurance, he continued and pushed the door open.

This room was just as he remembered it, just as he had left it all those many years ago. The curtains were open, welcoming the sunny winter day. The windows were still intact, and the brightly lit room still smelled like his mother, those comforting fragrances of perfume and incense that he could always associate with her. Memories and emotions flooded over him, threatening to drown him, and he wept.

On that familiar floor, where he had played as a child, Thor cried. He cried for all he had lost. He cried for his mother and her sacrifice for a reprieve that now would never be. He cried for himself and all the years of fear, pain, and loneliness. And through it all, the rose glowed, radiating its soft light and, with it, a sense of love and comfort.

It was some time before he could stand, but, eventually, he did, and, in this room, holding his mother's essence, he felt a sense of serenity and peace, that this was where she needed to be. Stepping over to the fireplace, he set the rose on the mantel where it began, slowly, to rotate.

After a moment, when he was sure the rose was okay, Thor returned to the old living room and picked up the broken piece of stem. Looking at it lying on the palm of his hand, he considered what to do with it, and, after some deliberation, he decided to bury it. He had not been able to send his mother off on a pyre and to mourn his loss. In one sense, it was like she were still with him; he spent endless hours talking to the rose as if to his mother, as if she were not gone at all. But in another sense, he knew she was gone, even if her essence and her spirit were now contained within this rose. His mother, who had held him and talked with him, was gone forever. He could burn this twig now, but somehow, burying her, even just this small piece of stem, seemed right, like laying her to rest.

The ground in the front courtyard was frozen solid, but he was determined. This had been her favorite place, where she sat in the sun, watched him play, and even joined in his childish games. This, he was certain, was where she would want her final resting place to be. So, he dug, tearing his fingers and breaking his claws against the frozen dirt, until he was satisfied with the depth. Ever so gently, he lifted the stem in his bloody hands and tenderly laid her in the hole. His tears fell freely into the dirt as he scooped handful after handful upon the tiny stem. Even after the work was done, Thor remained by the little grave long into the night.

In the weeks that followed, despite the frost and frozen earth, a single green sprout appeared and began to grow. Not just to grow, but to thrive. The sprout became a stalk which grew leaves and budded. Even in the dead of winter, it blossomed with radiant roses, which, in time, withered and died, only to be replaced by fresh new buds. Lovingly, Thor tended this bush which continued to grow and spread until the whole courtyard was a bright rose garden.

Over the next few years, it was as if his mother's essence had permeated the cursed woods. It lost its bloodlust. Her love had weakened its will, and, though it still fought off intruders, no longer was it intent on killing. Now it sought to drive them out by less lethal means: snares and thickets, mud and rash-causing plants. To enter was miserable and dangerous, but no longer as deadly. He wondered if anyone ever even tried anymore, if there were any chance he might yet find love, or if he was damned to this accursed form forever.

The dark woods still served its purpose; it still kept most people from finding the castle.

Hilde refused to cry as she walked among the bodies that lay in the blood-soaked snow. Absently brushing back loose strands of her fire-red hair, she surveyed the carnage of the Beast's most recent slaughter. This time, it was personal. She stepped over the body of a little girl to get a better look at the four perfect slashes across her brother's chest. They were identical to all the rest; four long, clean cuts, side by side, had killed all eight of the travelers returning from a nearby clanhold to celebrate the winter solstice.

She looked from one of her brothers to the other. Both died fighting; their weapons, still clutched in their cold dead hands, bore the blood of their enemy, a testament to their courage and warrior prowess. "They died a good death," she said, but that knowledge did little to soothe the heartache she felt.

Her father, Erik, nodded. "Yes, a good death."

He looked haggard. His wife had died eight years ago, taking a piece of him with her. He found the strength to go on in his love for his children. Then the accidental deaths of Hilde's little brother and sister two years ago had cut their family nearly in half and took another part of him. Afterward, their family of four had grown even closer, depending more and more on each other. She feared for her father now: his last two sons lying dead in the road, senselessly butchered.

Of course, everyone knew this road was dangerous, bordering, as it did, the Beast's dark woods, but it was the only road through the pass to other clanholds in the east where they sold and traded furs and crops. They also knew the story of the prince who had been damned by the gods and transformed into a monster, and that to enter the dark woods was to risk one's very life. It was the Beast's domain, and he killed anyone who entered it. The road had always been safe, as long as those who traversed it remained on the road and didn't enter the woods itself, but that had changed recently. Over the past few months, individuals, as well as small bands of travelers, had been killed, despite never leaving the road, always by the Beast's wicked claws, leaving deep gashes in the dead bodies.

"This is the first time the Beast has attacked a group so large," her father said to his friend, Ilya, stepping carefully around the bodies to survey the scene. Erik was a broad, burly man with arms and legs the size of small tree trunks. His fiery red hair—like Hilde's—hung down his back, and he wore a big bushy beard, lightly streaked with gray that hung over his barrel-like chest. Usually tall and proud, his shoulders were slumped forward, beaten down by the weight of his grief. Kneeling on the cold, frozen ground, with his huge, meaty hands, hard and calloused by years of work and years of war, he tenderly closed the dead, empty eyes of his younger son Haaken.

"He's growing bolder," Ilya agreed.

"If he'll attack a group of this size," Erik said with concern, "how long until he leaves the woods entirely and attacks us in our homes?"

Hilde stopped listening to the men. For a moment, she knelt beside Leif, her older brother. She brushed the brown hair from his pale, blood-speckled face and looked into those empty, milky eyes, then closed them and kissed his forehead. "Can we just get them home, please?"

All eyes turned to her. She saw their pity, and anger flared within her. "We know who or what killed them. It's no mystery. I don't want my brothers lying in the road any longer."

"Easy, Hilde. We'll get them home," Ilya assured her softly, reaching for her arm. "Come on, I'll ..."

Standing up, she spun on him and slapped his hand away. "No! I'm not going anywhere."

Ilya took a step back and nodded. "Okay. Okay. Take it easy."

Despite his sorrow, Erik smiled at the ferocity in her bright emerald eyes. He came over and spoke gently. "There's nothing more to be done here. When the wagons arrive, we'll bring them. Go home."

"But, Father ..."

He cut her off. "Don't argue, Hilde. Go home and get things ready. There's work to be done."

She nodded, knowing what he meant. For a moment, father and daughter gazed into each other's eyes. Neither spoke. There were no words, but in that moment, they shared something, an unspoken understanding.

As her father had ordered, Hilde walked home. She passed the wagons on her way, and, knowing that her brothers would be brought home soon, she got right to work. Filling buckets of water at the well, carrying them into the cottage, and covering the beds with thick cloths kept her busy until the sound of hooves and cartwheels in crunching snow announced their return.

As Leif's and Haaken's bodies were brought in and each laid out on their own bed, a couple of village women came to offer their help, but Hilde shook her head and closed the door. Two years ago, she had prepared her little brother and sister for the pyres; now, she would prepare Leif and Haaken. It was something she had to do by herself, her way of saying goodbye. Alone, she set to work, removing their clothes and washing her brothers' bodies. She fought down the tears that threatened to overcome her and focused on the task before her. "No," she chastised herself. "You can cry when that monster is dead."

This wasn't like the last times. She had washed those bodies too, but they had died of illness. These two had been murdered, and there was so much blood, so much dirt and crusted blood that stubbornly refused to wash away.

When they were finally clean, she struggled to dress them in their finest clothes and the warm, rabbit fur vests that she had given them. She remembered hiding the vests and diligently working in secret, only by candlelight, after the others had all gone to sleep. She had wanted them to be a surprise, and they had been. The smiles on her brothers' faces were worth every hour of lost sleep and every pricked finger. Once they were dressed, she combed their hair. She even combed Haaken's tuft of beard that she had teased him about but of which he was so proud.

When they were ready, she opened the door and admitted the men who would carry Leif and Haaken to the pyre that had been built while she was busy washing them. Eight pyres lined the lake's shore, each bearing the body of someone she knew, a friend, each butchered by the same preternatural monster. As the fires were lit and pushed into the water, on their last journey, Hilde settled the matter in her heart; she would kill the Beast. The pyres floated away with the water licking at the flames. Hilde felt her father behind her, his thick arms wrapped around her protectively. They stood together until the pyres had disappeared, the last of the flames sinking under the water's surface.

It was customary, after a death, to go to the Mead Hall, the center of village life, where everyone came together for merriment and mourning. At times like this, they gathered to share memories of loved ones and drink until they could no longer stand, but neither Hilde nor her father felt like attending. Instead, they walked home together, nibbled at a meal of bread and stew, and quietly kept each other company. Neither spoke much. They didn't need to. They drew their meager comfort from each other's presence.

Her father had never appeared old to her, but now, sitting across the table after the loss of his last two sons, his eyes bore the weight of his years.

Their cottage wasn't much, but it was home. It was one room, large by village standards, about eight paces square. Four beds, covered by warm furs, dominated one side of the room. On the other side were the fire pit, food storage, and a table that had once held seven. There were only four chairs now, and two of them sat empty. It didn't feel like home at all; it felt empty, foreign.

The day's events had been exhausting, but when, at last, Hilde lay down, sleep eluded her. Closing her eyes, she saw her dead brothers, saw their torn and bloody bodies. When sleep did come, it was a troubled sleep. In her dreams, Leif and Haaken called out from beyond, crying out for vengeance.

She woke in a cold sweat. The idea of closing her eyes again was terrifying, and so, for what felt like hours, she stared at the ceiling in the dark cottage. If he were here, Leif would have woken. He always woke when she had bad dreams. He would have snuggled up to her and put his arms around her, gently pulling her close and whispering something reassuring. She could have slept then; she could always sleep in his protective arms. But he wasn't there; he was dead. A single tear trickled from her eye before she could stop it, but she managed to fight down the rivers that threatened to overwhelm her. Eventually, exhaustion overcame her, and she lost consciousness into a deep dreamless sleep.

She woke again to her father's gentle touch. "Hilde."

"Father?" She could tell it was still before dawn. "Where are you going?" she asked, seeing his weapons and armor. Before he could answer, she knew and bounded from her bed, instantly awake. "I'm coming too!"

"No, you're not," he said, grabbing her arm.

"Yes, I am," she argued defiantly, yanking her arm away and pulling her jerkin over her head.

Her father took her arm again, but gently this time. "I need you to stay here, Hilde."

"I can fight!"

"Don't I know it!" He smiled at her and brushed her head with his hand. "I need you to stay here. There's a lot to be done, and I'll be gone for justa few days.

"But ..."

He cut her off. "Hilde, you're so headstrong. I tell you to do something, and you do the opposite, but I need you to listen this time. For once, just do what I say."

She recognized the hard edge in his voice, something he rarely used with her. "You're all I have left," she whispered, fighting to keep control.

He kissed her on the forehead and smiled. "And I'll be back in just a few days, but I need you to stay here and mind the house. The goats don't feed and milk themselves."

Reluctantly, Hilde nodded. Steadily, she looked him in the eye. "Three days."

Her father nodded. "Three days."

She watched as he gathered up his supplies and headed out the door. After hurriedly fastening her belt around her waist, Hilde followed him out of the village and watched him disappear into the Beast's dark woods.

As the days passed, Hilde did as she had promised and took care of the house and animals. She quickly learned that her father had not told even his closest friends of his intentions to enter the woods and hunt the Beast. When visitors came by to ask after him, she simply said he had gone hunting. This worked for the first few days, but soon people began to suspect this was more than just a hunting trip.

"Hunting, my ass," Ilya grunted, following her inside where she dropped an armful of logs by the fireplace. "If he went hunting, I'll bet I can guess what he's after."

"He'll be home soon," Hilde said, dismissing the big man's sarcasm while attempting to hide her own concerns.

"That damned fool!"

Hilde spun on him with fury in her eyes and started to advance. "Fool?" she spat. "My father is twice the man you are."

"Okay," he said, lifting his hands defensively. "Take it easy. I shouldn't have said that, I know, but going after the Beast alone is madness."

"Not madness, courage," she snapped, "and, if you weren't such a coward, you'd be there at his side right now."

Ilya's eyes narrowed. "I know you've been through a lot recently, but I'm no coward, and I'll not be called one by the likes of you."

Ilya was her father's best friend. They had shared life's greatest joys and deepest sorrows. Of the same height and build as Erik, Ilya was often mistaken as his brother. The only real dissimilarity was Ilya's raven black hair and beard that had yet to show any sign of gray. Hilde knew he was no coward, knew he had fought bravely by her father's side on many occasions, but, at this point, she was afraid for her father and angry. "Coward."

A big man, he brought his hand around with a blow that should have sent her sprawling. Though he was bigger, she was faster, ducking his strike and countering with a punch of her own that caught him squarely on the nose.

"So brave," she yelled, grabbing the fire poker, ready to deliver a painful blow. "Then why aren't you with him now?"

Ilya held his nose to stop the flow of blood. His eyes softened. "Because he didn't ask me."

For a moment, Hilde just looked at him. Sadness filling her eyes, she slowly lowered the poker, dropped it, then ran into the big man's arms and held on tight. Ilya had many times proven himself a brave and loyal friend, having followed Erik into many dangerous fights. Deep down, she knew that, if her father had asked, Ilya would have gone with him, even to his death.

As the big man held her, Hilde refused to cry, even though her voice betrayed her emotions. "He'll come home soon," she repeated, trying to convince herself

As time went on, while no one dared to suggest to her that he was dead, many offered looks of pity and sympathy, and urged her to come and live with them—just until her father came home. She always refused, insisting that he would be home soon and she needed to have the house in order for his return.

When, after two weeks, Erik had still not returned, Hilde made a decision: she was going to find him. Knowing they would try to stop her, she told no one of her intentions, and, in the early morning with a full moon low over the horizon, before any but the earliest risers were even awake, she stood in the dimly lit and empty house. Her thick leather jerkin, the only armor she wore, was cinched tight around her waist by a well-worn leather belt with a loop from which hung the deadly hand-axe her father had given her when she received her sacred arm-ring and became a shield maiden. Leif's antler-handled knife hung in its sheath on her other hip. An inverted flame of braided hair hung down her back, keeping it away from her fierce green eyes, eyes that bore a hatred as icy as a frost giant's heart.

After one last glance around the house that no longer felt like home, Hilde donned her thick warm cloak and stepped out into the pre-dawn chill, swearing an oath to rescue her father and kill the monster that had left her home and her heart so void of the life and the love they once knew.

At the tree line, she stopped. Fog leaked from the dark woods like snakes slithering to hide among the winter-barren shrubs bordering it. It was a sinister place, and she imagined what horrors she might find within its depths.

For a moment, she hesitated, then realized she had stopped because she was frightened. Angry at herself, she growled and plunged into the woods, the fog parting and swirling around her. The trees were darker than in other forests, the undergrowth denser under the thick layer of snow. Even as she trudged on, her feet seemed to tangle with every step. The sounds were strange too. The sounds themselves were the same: small creatures scurrying on the ground and among the branches, but it was like these sounds were being made in a vacuum. It all just seemed somehow wrong.

Deeper into the woods, a cold wind blew through the trees, and she wrapped her cloak a little tighter. Somehow, despite the snow and below-freezing temperature, the earth was soggy. It was still early morning, the sun was just climbing over the horizon, when the ground, which had appeared solid a moment before, shifted beneath her boots, sending her sprawling down a small hill. Cursing, she pushed herself to her feet on snow and frozen dirt, only to find, as she stood, that her boots were sinking into thick mud. Hilde tried to step out but couldn't pull her feet free.

Fear took over, and adrenaline surged. She grabbed hold of a small tree and pulled, yanking her legs up as she hauled herself out of the muddy sinkhole. Still holding to the tree out of desperation, she gulped in deep breaths of air and tried to stop her hands from trembling, tried to calm down. These woods terrified her; she wanted to leave, just to get out, but her father was in here. She couldn't leave without him.

Minutes passed as she breathed and steeled herself, then, trying to stand, she found her feet tangled in a web of vines and roots. Again, fear welled up inside her. She yanked and kicked, but the entanglements only tightened. Fighting down her growing panic, she stopped struggling, took a breath and thought about what to do. Kicking wasn't working; she had to cut the vines and roots. An easy answer, she thought, drawing Leif's knife and freeing herself. Easy, yes, but only easy if she kept her head. Fear and panic were deadly here.

Hilde continued on, staying close to trees, just in case she needed to grab one, should the ground give out beneath her. A terrifying prospect. She knew, from the position of the sun, that she was moving in the right direction, but the ground was so confusing. It felt like everything was constantly changing and shifting. She had to keep an eye on the sky because to watch the ground was to become turned around, was to find herself heading back out with the sun on the wrong side.

Carefully watching the sky, she moved deeper yet into the woods, using a stick to test the ground before each step. She quickly abandoned the idea after the stick reported solid ground under the snow, but her feet sank into mud in the same spot.

Watching the ground for danger and the sky for guidance was difficult and dangerous. A glance upward, taking her eyes off the woods and the ground, meant risking her footing, maybe her life.

When the sun had reached its apex, Hilde had been turned around more times than she could count and was beginning to wonder if she'd ever find her father. She had yet to find any trace of him or the Beast. But then, as she crested a hill, there it was, the massive stone wall of a fortified clanhold: the Beast's lair. The stone walls were covered in thick moss and vines, but it was easily discernible as the Beast's castle. The turrets and the windows of the sinister structure's second story were empty, ghostly. A curtain fluttered in the wind outside a broken window like the dress of a corpse dancing on the strings of a marionette.

Moving constantly, so her feet wouldn't sink in the snow-covered mud, Hilde crept along the wall, which was surprisingly still intact and impregnable. The wall that hid her also hid the Beast. That monster was around somewhere, she knew, and she did not want to get caught off guard. Ears alert to any sound, eyes scanning her surroundings, she moved quickly and quietly until she reached the entrance. The massive ironbound gates were open wide, inviting to his death anyone who ventured beyond.

She stopped and peered around the corner. It was an empty, desolate place. Torn curtains blew out through broken windows. The walkways were covered with snow and ice. Walking through the gates was like walking into Niflheim itself. The grounds were neglected and forgotten, except for a beautiful courtyard garden which, even now in the dead of winter, was alive with bright pink rosebushes.

Amazed, Hilde took a few steps, inexplicably drawn toward the flowers, but stopped and chastised herself. She was not here to look at roses, fascinating as they were; she was here to find her father and to kill that murderous Beast.

But had her father even made it here? Had he survived the woods: the sinkholes, ensnaring vines, and the ease by which one lost his way? She pushed these thoughts from her mind and, keeping a wary eye on her surroundings, walked up the thick stone stairs to the castle's ironbound doors. Of course, he had made it. She cursed herself for even doubting it; he had trained her, and she had made it. He had too. The door was ajar and looked like it had been for a long time.

He was in here, and he needed her, she told herself as she slipped through the door into the dimly lit grand entrance. It was mostly dark. Years of dirt and grime caked the now snow-covered windows, allowing few shafts of sunlight to penetrate its murky gloom. She stayed close to the wall, listening for any sign of danger. The old castle creaked and groaned. Her head spun at every sound, but there was nothing, only the sounds of an old rundown house and the wind howling through its empty halls. She started on the first floor, creeping from room to room, looking for any sign of her father, but she found nothing, just a lot of unkempt rooms, many of which were brightly lit by the sun streaming in through broken windows and glistening off snow-dusted floors.

A staircase wound down, deep into the bowels of this monster's lair. She hesitated but refused her fear and forced herself to descend step after step into this unholy abyss. At the bottom, the darkness and coolness sent a chill up her spine, but Hilde pushed on. Barely able to see more than a few feet in front of herself and hearing the skittering of rats and who knew what else, she made her way along the wall into dark room after dark room, rooms long abandoned: storage rooms for food and grain, for castle supplies of all kinds.

The darkness thickened as she continued, and she began to question the wisdom of going deeper, but then she heard something. At first, her adrenaline surged as she thought of where she could hide, but she forced herself to calm down. She refused to allow panic to overcome reason. The sound was deeper down the corridor. Standing still, listening, she took a few deep breaths to steel her courage. It wasn't getting any closer. She moved slowly toward the sound. It wasn't growling; it was coughing. She recognized that cough.

Desperate, hope made her rash, and she ran the last distance of corridor, pushed her way through the slightly open big ironbound door, and burst into the somewhat brighter dungeon. Cells, lit by small, barred windows, lined either side of this dead-end hall, and an icy breeze ran a chill up her spine. There in the first cell, behind a door of rusty iron bars, sitting against the wall, was the man she had risked it all to find.

"Father!" Hilde cried, running to the bars and reaching for him. "You're alive!"

He struggled slowly to his feet, and, using the wall for balance, stumbled his way to the door. Awkwardly, he embraced her through the bars and cried.

Hilde had never seen her father cry. "I'm going to get you out of here."

"No," he said, getting a hold of himself, "No, Hilde, my dear. You must go."

"I will, just as soon as I get you out. We'll go together."

"Stop, Hilde." He coughed, drawing her attention. "I never dreamed I'd see you again. You've made me a very happy man, but you can't stay. You can't be here when he returns. Please go!"

"I'm not going anywhere until I get you out of here," she argued, pulling away and yanking on the cell door.

"Hilde."

"No!" Looking him hard in the eye, Hilde snapped, "I'm not leaving!"

Seeing her determination, he grunted. "You're just like your mother."

Her face split into a big grin as she set to work on the lock. Her dagger wouldn't fit into the keyhole. She retrieved her father's crossbow bolt from where the Beast had carelessly tossed Erik's gear into the corner of the room, but it wouldn't fit either. Nor would anything else she could think of until she tried the prong from the buckle on her belt. It fit easily into the keyhole but lacked the leverage to move the mechanism.

"Damn!" she swore in frustration, refastening the belt around her waist.

"It's okay, Honey. You tried, and I appreciate ..." he began, but her glare silenced him.

"I'm not leaving!"

"Hilde."

Noise from down the hall drew their attention. "You have to hide, Hilde."

"I'll stand and fight. I'll ..."

84

"No!" He coughed. "Damn it, girl. Listen to me." When he had her full attention, he demanded, "You will hide. You will wait until he leaves, and then we'll get you out of here."

"Fine. I'll hide," she spat. "But I'm not leaving." She grabbed Erik's heavy crossbow and quiver and hurried down the corridor. Not wanting to step foot in a cell, she hid behind an old overturned table. After cranking the crossbow and setting a bolt, she crouched down out of sight and listened. There was barely any sound until the big door to the dungeon creaked open on its rusty hinges.

"What are you going to do with me, Beast?"

A deep guttural voice responded, "Eat."

"What do you want?" Erik asked. "Why haven't you killed me yet?"

"Would you prefer I kill you?"

"I would prefer you release me."

"So you can drive that big axe of yours into my skull?"

"Yes."

For a moment, there was silence, then a strange, loud sniffing sound.

"Come out," the Beast called.

"Are you mad, Beast?" her father cried out from his cell.

"I can smell your sweat and fear," the Beast said, ignoring him. "Now come out."

Shrugging out of her warm fur-lined cloak to allow herself ease of movement, Hilde rose to her feet and leveled her father's crossbow at the Beast. She saw a hideous caricature of a wolf standing upright, well over two meters tall. Thick brown fur covered his body from head to toe. Long sharp claws tipped humanlike fingers and canine hind paws. "Unlock the door and let my father out."

His lip curled back, exposing long yellow fangs, but whether in a smirk or a snarl was hard to tell. "No," he said, clearly and flatly.

"Do it, or I'll kill you and do it myself."

Without any warning and faster than Hilde could register, the beast lunged to one side. She spun and loosed the bolt, but missed; it clanged harmlessly off the stone wall mere inches from the Beast. Even before it clacked to a stop on the floor, the Beast had shoved off the wall, hurling himself toward her. Dropping the crossbow, she reached for her axe but was too late. He was on her before she could lift it.

His toothy maw just inches from her face, the Beast snarled, spraying spittle across her face. With one fierce yank, he tore the axe from her grasp, sending it clanking across the floor.

Refusing to accept defeat, Hilde reached for Leif's knife, but the Beast wasn't done. Before she could clear the blade, he grabbed the front of her belt and jerkin, slid her across the floor into a cell, and slammed the barred door.

Hilde sprang to her feet to face the Beast, adrenaline surging through her veins. He only offered a toothy grin and said, "There! That should hold you."

"I'm going to kill you, Beast," Hilde spat defiantly.

Without another word, he turned and picked up the crossbow and axe from the floor. After hanging them on hooks at the end of the corridor, he nudged the plate of food he had entered with closer to her father's cell and left, pulling the oversized door partly closed behind him.

With the Beast gone, her father leaned against the bars of his cell door and said, "I told you. You should have left."

"I'm not leaving."

"Not anymore, no."

She was quiet for a moment, then asked, "Since when do you give up?" Met only with silence, she continued, "That monster may have won this round, but he hasn't beaten me."

"You're in a cage," her father reminded her.

"But I'm not dead," she spat angrily. "And as long as I'm alive, I'll fight."

Her defiance was met with only silence, and this worried her. Erik was a fierce, brave warrior. He had single-handedly held men together who were ready to flee. His strength and courage had inspired and rallied them, so they had eventually carried the day. She had never known him to give up any fight.

"What happened, Father?" she asked. "How did you wind up in this dungeon?"

She heard him grunt, and, as she awaited the response she knew would be forthcoming, Hilde set to work trying to find a way out of her cell. It was reasonably large, about seven paces deep and four wide. At the back, secured to the wall, was a chain, ending in a metal circlet which could be locked around a person's neck. She shivered at the thought before continuing her search. Aside from the chain, a layer of dust, and rat droppings, the cell was empty.

"You came through them, so you know what those cursed woods are like," he began as she tinkered with the lock to no avail. "I almost got swallowed by the earth a dozen times …" He stopped and coughed before continuing his story. "Vines entangled my feet and legs, so I narrowly escaped a horrible death. Every time I thought I had made some progress, I found myself blazing a trail in the wrong direction."

"I know what that's like," Hilde agreed, examining the hinges. Then using her belt knife, she scraped at them and tried to find a way to remove the center pin.

"I barely reached the castle before nightfall. I dread what evils roam those woods under cover of darkness."

Hilde hadn't thought of that. The idea made her shudder, and she was very glad to have gotten through as quickly as she had. The hinges wouldn't budge, so she examined the bars, looking at the rust for any signs of weakness she could exploit.

"I came upon an old overgrown road, which I followed right up to the castle's front gate. No one was around, but I moved carefully, expecting that monster to jump out at any second. There was still no sign of him. The castle was overgrown and deserted. The windows were like the eyes of a warrior after the Valkyries have carried his soul to Valhalla. But when I came into the courtyard, I found something very different and out of place."

"The rose garden," Hilde said, remembering how its beauty had attracted her, and was distracted even now as she thought of it.

Her father's cough returned her focus. The bars were solid, with a little rust, but not enough to weaken them. Stepping back, she realized that the bars were not all uniform. They were unevenly spaced. Some of the gaps between them were narrow, but some were fairly wide.

Hilde had been teased relentlessly for being small and skinny. She was also wiry and deceptively strong and had made many boys twice her size regret their insults. Now as she listened to her father's story, she tried to squeeze out through the widest of the gaps.

"Yes, that damned cursed rose garden," he grumbled, after finishing another bout of coughing.

"Are you okay?"

"I'm fine," he growled and returned to his story. "I was surprised to see such beauty in this wretched place. It was so unnatural. Foolishly, I went over for a closer look and was amazed to find that the roses were actually glowing. Curious, I reached for one and snapped the stem. Immediately, the whole bush of roses began to shake with the chiming sound of little bells. Then I heard something else, something crashing through the underbrush, and, before I could crank my crossbow and load a bolt, the Beast charged through the gate and into the courtyard. Dropping my crossbow, I drew my axe, planning to split that monster's skull."

When he paused and did not go on, Hilde, who had her head and shoulders out through the bars but couldn't get the rest of herself through, asked, "What happened?" She could almost fit, but, push as she might, the gap was just too small.

"That wily monster stopped, then began to move with slow lumbering steps. I prepared for his attack, but what came caught me completely off guard. The slowness was an act; when he came, he came in quickly, lunging in faster than I thought possible. I swung but was too late. He was already upon me. I tried to fight, but he clubbed me on the head, and, when I woke up, I was right here in this cell."

"So why the hell hasn't he killed us?" Hilde asked, trying again to squeeze through the bars from a different angle. She was so close, but, just barely, couldn't get through.

"I don't know. I've asked, but he never answers," her father responded before beginning another coughing fit.

Having heard that raw cough before, Hilde know it wasn't good. Unfastening her belt and peeling the thick leather jerkin over her head. "Well, I see he's at least feeding you."

"Yeah, if you can call it food," he answered with another cough. "He brings me plates of barely cooked meat, usually still saturated in blood," he finished before another coughing fit.

After stripping off her clothes, her bare skin covered in goosebumps, Hilde tried again to force her way between the bars. Now, without that extra layer, finally, painfully, she fit. She fished her clothes out through the bars and redressed, then went to her father's cell wearing a big sly grin. The grin disappeared quickly, however, when the dim light from the small window revealed him on the floor, leaning against the cold stone wall. He was pale and sickly, like he had aged ten years in the hour since she had arrived.

"Father?"

"I'm fine," he coughed, getting up and crossing to the barred door. "How did you get out?"

"I squeezed between the bars." She offered a weak smile and felt his forehead. He was burning up. "I just barely fit, but I'm out. I'm going to find the key."

"No," he said, grabbing her arm in a death grip. "You're going to get out of here."

"I'm not leaving you." She yanked away, surprised and afraid of how fragile his grip was.

"Damn it, girl! Yes, you are," he said and began another bout of coughing. "You've got a second chance. Now you're going to sneak up out of here and go home."

"I'm going to sneak up out of here," she began, repeating his words, then continued with her own, "find the key and get you out of ..."

"Hilde!"

"Shh," she hushed him with a finger to her lips. "Keep it down. Drawing his attention is not going to help either of us."

"Please, Hilde," he begged. "Please just go home."

"I'm not going home without you." She spun on her heels and walked down the corridor to where their weapons hung on the wall. Grabbing her crossbow and axe, she turned back toward the entrance.

"Hilde," he coughed.

"I'll be back to let you out in just a little while," she insisted, slipping through the mostly closed door and jogging as quietly as she could down the hall. At the bottom of the narrow staircase, she stopped and cranked the crossbow string back before setting a bolt and starting her ascent. She was alert, watching and listening for any sign of her quarry.

At the top of the stairs, she stopped, hoping to hear something, anything that would indicate where to look. There was only silence, so she crept, quietly as she could, from one room to another. The furniture, or what was left of it, was piled against the wall; curtains whipped around in wind that blew through broken windows. What were once plush carpets on the floors and elegant tapestries adorning the walls had been long neglected and were now torn and moth-eaten.

In the Grand Foyer, she heard a noise, not the sound of wind and whipping curtains, but a thump. It came from upstairs. Ascending the once ornate staircase, she ran on her toes to soften her steps. She crouched at the top, peeking around the corner. Hearing another thump, she jerked back, then slowly, cautiously, hazarded another peek. She didn't see anyone, didn't see anything except a strange pink glow at the end of the hall. Still, she didn't move, just watched. But time passed, and she saw no sign of the Beast. Warily, she crept around the banister and down the hall toward the eerie pink glow.

Thump.

Hilde pressed her back to the wall. Her heart was pounding. Adrenaline surged as she leveled the crossbow. The sound had come from the room to her right. She gathered her courage again and inched closer and closer. The door was closed. She reached for the knob and turned it, expecting, at any second, for the Beast to jump out and attack her. The knob turned. Holding on with one hand, with the crossbow up against her shoulder, she took one deep steadying breath and shoved. The door was stuck, then popped and screeched open, crashing into the wall as she dropped the heavy crossbow into her empty hand. Her eyes darted around the dark room, but she saw no sign of the monster.

Thump.

She spun toward the sound, ready to let fly a killing bolt, but she was alone in the room. A rocking chair swung back and forth with the wind streaming through a broken window and gusts strong enough to rock it into the wall.

Thump.

Lowering the bow and shaking her head, she sighed, then stood stock still. The hair on the back of her neck stood up, and she knew he was right behind her. For a second, she didn't dare to move, just waited for the fatal blow to land. Seconds passed, and it didn't come. Swallowing the lump in her throat, she made her decision and snapped into action. Dropping to one knee, she spun and loosed the bolt.

Nothing. No cry of pain. No flurry of claws and teeth. Just the dull thud of her bolt burying itself into the wood paneling across the hall. She expelled a deep breath as a tear trickled down her cheek, a tear of relief. The Beast wasn't behind her as she had feared, but this was still his lair, and he could be around any corner.

With a bit of work, Hilde yanked the bolt from the wall. It would have been a dead giveaway that she had been there. She then closed the door and crept on down the hall toward the room with the pink glow. Granted, she had just shot a crossbow bolt into the wall, which should have drawn the attention of anyone so close, but just in case he was in there, she cranked the string and loaded the bolt again.

She reached the room at the end of the hall. The door stood open, and, as she looked inside, she was surprised to find a commodious sitting room. It was the first room she had seen that wasn't neglected or in ruins. On the contrary, this one was comfortable and inviting: thick carpets lay neatly on the floor, plush pillows of all colors sat on luxurious sofas and chairs.

The windows were intact, framed by velvet curtains. The walls were clean and bore beautiful paintings. In here, she felt a sense of warmth and comfort that she had sensed nowhere else in this wretched place. But what drew her attention, what amazed her was, on the mantle of the fireplace, a single pink rose from which emanated a soft pink glow. It hovered an inch above the mantle, slowly turning, and, oddly, it had only one petal remaining.

With a whole garden of pink roses in the courtyard, Hilde wondered why this one, having lost most of its petals, was here, displayed so elegantly. As she reached for the rose, she stopped and snatched her hand back. Her father had warned her about touching the roses.

Looking around, she was surprised to find that she had crossed the room. So transfixed was she by the rose that she didn't even realize she had moved from the doorway, that she had crossed the room and nearly made a fatal mistake.

Hilde backed toward the door. Movement outside caught her eye, and, as she looked out the window, she saw the Beast returning from the woods, a large deer slung around his neck. He held it by its forefeet on one side and its hind feet on the other.

Standing stock still, Hilde hoped he wouldn't notice her. Once he was out of sight of the window, she hurriedly slipped from the comfortable sitting room, leaving everything exactly as she had found it. Quickly, but quietly, she ran down the hall toward the stairs. A loud grunt signaled the Beast's entrance and stopped Hilde dead before she reached the stairs to take up her position. She heard him muttering to himself and the sound of his claws click-clacking on the pristine marble floor. She concentrated, listening for the distinctive sounds that would signal his approach and glancing around for a place to hide if he came up. Numerous doors lined the hall, but she feared that they had not been opened in so long that they might be swollen shut or creak loudly when opened, giving her away.

The click-clack of his footsteps faded, however, and Hilde relaxed a little. She crept ahead and peered down the stairs. The Beast was nowhere in sight. "Where did you go?" she wondered, descending the stairs as fast and as silently as possible. He had not come up, so he was either on the first floor or down in the dungeon. If he were in the dungeon, then he would soon know she was loose. Would that endanger her father? She didn't know, but he would certainly begin hunting for her.

A noise drew her attention, not from the dungeon, but from this floor. Hugging the wall with her crossbow at the ready, she made her way in the direction of the sound. Her heart threatened to beat its way right out of her chest, and her breathing, though she tried to control it, was loud in her own ears. The noise, however, persisted, and she hoped that indicated he was unaware of her approach.

Drawing closer, she could hear his deep, gravelly voice complaining about having to cook food. She peered around the corner into the kitchen. There the Beast stood, grumbling incoherently. He had started a fire in the open fireplace against the wall and was preparing the deer for the spit. For a moment, she just watched as he gutted and skinned it. Then, to her disgust, with a sickening crack, he tore a hind leg from the carcass and took a big, bloody bite of the raw meat.

Hilde gagged as she tasted bile but fought down the urge to vomit. Swallowing hard, she continued to watch her quarry, biding her time, waiting for her opportunity.

Finally, she saw it. As the Beast leaned in to set the spitted deer in place over the fire, she struck, hoping to catch him off-guard. Quickly, she ran in, leveled the crossbow, and let fly the deadly bolt. Hilde's aim was perfect. The bolt flew true toward the Beast's exposed side under his right arm, a perfect kill shot.

With preternatural reflexes, the Beast twisted his body, so the bolt missed its mark. Instead, it carved a deep gash across his chest. He howled in pain. Before she could reload, he had turned toward her and was ready.Cursing, Hilde dropped the crossbow and yanked her axe free. It was smaller than her father's but no less deadly.

As they faced off, she spun the axe around in her hand, taking comfort in the feel of its weight and balance. The room filled with the Beast's deep guttural growl as they watched each other. Hoping to capitalize on the injury of her first strike, Hilde stepped in quickly, feigned right, and swung left toward the bolt's gash.

The Beast, however, was not fooled. He sidestepped the mighty blow, and, once the axe had finished its arc, stepped back in. Using his momentum against her, the Beast heaved Hilde across the room. She crashed into a table and went down but tucked into a roll and sprang back up and around to face him with feline grace.

Knowing she couldn't let him go on the offensive, Hilde pressed her attack, running in and swinging for his face. The blow was painfully deflected by a swat of his hand.Allowing the axe to continue in its arc, she turned in a full circle and brought the blade down toward the Beast's feet.

The Beast leapt over the wicked strike and kicked her in the head, sending Hilde sprawling across the floor. She tried to roll with it, but, before she could recover, he was on her. Her hand and half of the axe's handle disappeared into his massive grasp. Like a child's doll, he lifted her off the floor, high up into the air to dangle by her arm. Drawing her close, her face a mere six inches from his own, his lips curled back, and he uttered a low resonant growl.

Dizzy from the kick to her head, Hilde hung limply for a moment, but, instead of terrifying her, his sinister growl awakened something inside her. Invigorated, she punched him with her free hand and began to flail her legs, kicking him anywhere she could.

He thrust his arm out, extending her further from his body. She still kicked, but with far less success. Drawing Leif's knife from her belt, Hilde swung. The Beast was out of range for a critical hit, so she managed to inflict only a scratch. Before she could swing again, he had caught this hand too. With both hands captured, she redoubled her kicking, landing blow after blow, to which the Beast grunted in pain and frustration.

Nearly faster than she could register, he had both of her hands in one of his meaty fists, then he swung her, caught her feet in the other, and slung her around his neck, carrying her like the deer he had brought out of the woods. Now totally incapacitated, she stopped struggling and allowed herself to be carried back down to the dungeon.

As they entered, wakened by the commotion, her father saw her slung across the Beast's shoulders and started yelling curses and threats and pounding on the bars.

Ignoring him, the Beast looked at the cell he had locked her in, and seeing it still closed, grunted. He hesitated for a moment, then carried her to another cell. Without a word, he released her legs and swung her from his shoulders to dangle like a puppet. She reached for the floor, but her feet found only air. With his now free hand, the Beast yanked the weapon from her still clasped hands and tossed it down the hall before heaving her backward into the cell. He slammed the door with far more force than was necessary, with finality, then turned and stalked out of the room, fingering the gash across his chest and pulling the huge dungeon door fully closed behind him.

The room was silent after he left, even long after the sound of his footfalls receded into the emptiness of the cursed castle.

Eventually, the silence was broken by a fit of coughing.

"Father?" Hilde cried.

"I'm fine, child," he answered, trying to catch his breath. "You should have run."

Hilde dropped to the floor, leaned back against the cold stone wall, and closed her eyes. "I told you. I'm not leaving without you."

"You're so damned stubborn," he accused, then in a softer voice, he said, "Hilde, you tried. You did more than anyone could have expected, more than anyone could have hoped for, but …"

"I'm not leaving without you," she repeated.

"Hilde, be reasonable."

Unable to stem the flow of tears, she cried, "You're all I have left. Everyone else is already gone, and I'm not losing you too."

He was silent for a moment. "We have lost so much," he said softly. "But you staying here and dying with me won't accomplish anything. I can't get out, but if you can, then please, Hilde, let me die knowing that you are at home safe."

"You're not going to die," she insisted stubbornly. She heard him sigh in disappointment. "I'm going to take a nap, then, in the morning, I'll slip back out and go find him. I'll catch him when he's tired and unprepared. I'll kill him, unlock your cell, and together we'll go home."

She expected him to argue, but there was only the sound of his labored breath. He couldn't last long, already sick and trapped in a cold, damp cell. If he stayed, she knew, he would die. Her course decided, she lay down on the cold, bare floor with her head on her arms and closed her eyes.

Just as she started to doze off, she was jarred back awake as a metal plate was dropped on the floor in front of her father's cell. "It's burnt," the monster said, "but that's her fault." He then dropped another plate in front of her cell. For a moment, he stood staring at her.

"What?" she snapped.

Without another word, he turned and left the room.

Her father's plate scraped across the floor, then, a few seconds later, he said, "Burnt is a lot better than raw, and, since it's your fault, thank you."

She could hear the smile in his voice as he spoke those last words. It was great to hear that he could still jest.

She didn't want to give the Beast the satisfaction of eating his food, but she had to acknowledge it did smell good, and she was hungry. After a moment's indecision, she decided that the meat would give her the strength to kill her captor and took a bite. Refusing to admit that it really was good, she ate every scrap of meat. Then with a full belly, she lay down and closed her eyes.

When she woke, Hilde had no idea how much time had passed. Hearing her father's loud rhythmic snoring, she smiled. Even in this wretched place, that sound comforted her.

After standing and wiping the sleep from her eyes, she examined more closely the bars of this cell. Again, some spaces were wider than others, and she looked carefully for the widest gap. None were quite as wide as the one in her last cell, but she hoped that stubborn determination would help her force her way through.

Quickly she removed her belt and leather jerkin and tossed them on the floor by the bars. She closed her eyes for a moment to steel her resolve, then opened them and, with determination, slipped her arm and leg through the gap. Immediately she knew it would be a much tighter fit. After a deep breath, she exhaled as hard as she could and pushed herself between the bars. Her head and thigh slipped through, but her chest and bottom resisted. Try as she might, she just couldn't fit. The gap was just barely too narrow.

Frustrated, she stepped back into the cell but caught her foot on the bars and squealed in surprise as she stumbled backward and fell, her bottom landing squarely on the Beast's plate, right on the slimy fat left over from her meal.

"Are you okay?" Erik asked, his voice thick with worry.

Rolling out of the mess, she grimaced. "Eeew!" Trying to wipe it off only smeared it. "Yuck!" Disgust and frustration welled up inside and threatened to overcome her.

"Hilde?"

Feeling tears in her eyes, she blinked them away and pushed herself back up. "I'm fine."

"What happened?"

"I tripped and fell. I'm fine." The words came out harsher than she'd meant, and in the growing silence, she wiped her hand on a bar. Most of the grease came off, but it still left a slimy film that would not go away. She grabbed her clothes to wipe herself but stopped.

Grease!

Tossing her clothes back to the floor close to the bars, she scraped the plate with her fingers and began smearing it on the widest parts of her body: on her breasts, buttocks, and even her shoulder blades as best she could reach.

With grim determination, she walked back to the bars and looked again at the widest gap. Everything was on the line; not just her revenge, but her father's life depended on this moment. She had to get through.

Her jaws set, her course resolved, she slipped one leg into the gap, then pushed her head and shoulders through until it got tight. This is it, she told herself, then exhaled as hard as she could and pushed herself through the narrow gap. It was tight, and it hurt, but she gritted her teeth and pressed on as her greasy skin slid past the unyielding metal bars.

A whimper of pain escaped her lips as she kept pushing. She tried to take a breath but couldn't in the narrow confines of the bars. Desperately, she exhaled the tiny bit of air she had and tried to haul herself through the gap, tried to force the other breast past the bar.

She couldn't fit. Mustering her strength, she tried again but to no avail. Darkness began to creep around the edges of her vision, and her head started spinning.

Her father coughed.

That was the sound of his need, and it forced her back to consciousness. If she failed, he would die. She couldn't let that happen.

With one last effort, one desperate push, she planted her feet hard against the floor and shoved. Pain washed over her as the bar felt like razors against her greased breasts, but, still, she heaved and slid through.

Finally, past the bars, air filled her lungs as she gasped. She cupped her sore breasts, and even that was painful. Both, she saw, were red and raw, but she wasn't bleeding much, just scraped.

Unfortunately, her ordeal wasn't over. The top half of her body was free, but she still had to squeeze her bottom through. Gritting her teeth, she took a good hold on the bars, shifted her weight, and pushed with all her strength. The bars scraped across her body, but this time she had some leverage and was able to push through quickly, if painfully.

After just a moment to collect herself, Hilde reached through the bars for her clothes, wiped herself as best she could, and hurriedly got dressed. She recovered her axe and knife from down the hall where the Beast had thrown them, then went back to her father's cell where he still lay snoring. She considered waking him but thought better of it; he would only nag her to leave. Better to just let him sleep.

"I love you, Father," she whispered before heading to the dungeon door. This time the Beast had closed it. Hoping not to wake her father or alert the Beast, she grabbed the handle and pulled.

The door didn't budge.

She took a moment to prepare herself, took the handle in both hands and braced her feet against the jamb. Then, with all her strength, she pulled.

The door creaked and groaned before finally scraping open a few inches.

Stopping to take a few deep breaths and to glare at the door, Hilde cursed that monster who had swung it closed with such ease. Determined, she braced herself again and pulled, the heavy door creaking open a few more inches. It took longer than she would have liked, but, after a few more tries and a lot of effort, she opened the door wide enough. As she slipped through the crack, she could hear her father still snoring. She smiled.

In almost no time at all, she climbed the stairs and came out onto the first floor once again. Quickly, but stealthily, she crept from room to room, watching and listening for any sign of her quarry. In the kitchen, the site of their last battle, she found her father's crossbow, carelessly kicked aside from where she had dropped it. Its weight and feel in her hands were reassuring. Retrieving the bolt she had loosed the last time, she smiled at the bloody tip. If he bled, he could be killed. She recovered her father's quiver and reloaded the bolt before continuing her search.

After some time, she felt confident that the first floor was clear and made her way upstairs, ascending the same staircase she had used the last time. Almost immediately upon reaching the second floor, Hilde noticed the faint pink glow from the room at the end of the hall.

Slowly she made her way down, listening at each door as she passed. Then she heard it. She froze. The Beast's voice. From the end of the hall. The door stood ajar. He was talking to someone. She couldn't make out the words.

Realizing she was frozen in place by fear, she willed her legs to move, and, reluctantly, they obeyed. If the Beast were not alone, she thought, what would she do? Twice they had fought, and twice he had bested her. Again, she was relying on the element of surprise, but would surprise be enough if he had company? She doubted it.

She considered hiding and waiting until he was alone but dismissed the idea. Time was on his side; if she didn't act now, she might never get another chance.

Forcing herself forward, all the way to the door that stood ajar, allowed her a limited view of the room. Occasionally, the Beast was barely visible as he paced to and fro.

"… cooking. I don't like cooking," the Beast complained to someone Hilde couldn't see. "What am I going to do with them? Why won't they just leave me alone?"

No one responded.

"Oh, it's useless," he went on. "Why do I even bother?"

He was quiet for a moment, and Hilde crept through the door, toward the fireplace, hoping for a better vantage point from which to see the room and line up her shot.

"She's a feisty little thing," the Beast continued. "But why did she come here? Well, for her father, but why did he come here? Why do they want to kill me so badly?"

Seeing that he was indeed alone and talking to himself, Hilde leveled her crossbow and cried, "Cause you're a murderer!" and let fly the bolt.

The Beast spun toward her at the sound of her voice. The bolt hit its mark, driving deeply into his shoulder. He howled in pain, but instead of going down and allowing her to reload, he lunged forward, toward her.

Dropping the crossbow, Hilde drew her axe. He was almost on her, causing her to swing wildly. The Beast leaped aside and came around, following the blade, to shove her hard.

Recovering and regaining her feet, Hilde faced off against him. "Where's the key?" she demanded. "Where's the key to my father's cell?"

The Beast glanced at the rose, then back, but said nothing.

"Give me the key, Beast, or I shall kill you and find it myself." She swung a blow that he batted aside before landing a hard hit of his own to her chest. She stumbled backward and tripped, landing hard on the floor. He was on her then, her hand and axe pinned under his huge padded foot. As he raised his massive fist to deliver a final, fatal blow, she knew she was about to die. She turned to meet his eyes, defiantly accepting her fate.

Instead of blackness, however, there was a blinding flash of bright pink, and Hilde involuntarily squeezed her eyes shut against the glare. Her body was yanked to the side as her belt snapped free.

When she opened her eyes again, she saw the Beast standing a few feet away, whimpering like a puppy, as he pulled the crossbow bolt out of his shoulder. He turned to look at her, his face blank. Then he gazed at the rose, which still glowed brightly.

He turned back to her. "You want the key."

It wasn't a question, but she nodded anyway. Mustering her courage, she replied, "Give me the key, and I'll let you live."

The Beast laughed as he grimaced in pain. "You'll let …" The rose flared, cutting off his next words. He took a deep breath and steadied himself, then nodded. "I'll make a deal with you."

"I think my deal's fair," she said stubbornly, pushing her sore body to its feet. She reached for her knife, but both her knife and belt were gone.

The Beast smiled, a fiendish sight. "I relieved you of your knife," he said, then turned back to the matter at hand. "I will set your father free if you will remain here with me."

Hilde cocked her head curiously, then countered. "Let my father and me go, and we won't kill you."

"Very well," he scowled, "Back to the dungeon."

As he reached for her, she grabbed a fire poker, the only thing at hand, and swung, delivering a solid blow to his wounded shoulder.

Snarling in pain and rage, he lunged at her faster than she could react, tore the poker from her hand and threw it.

Hilde glanced around hurriedly for another weapon, any weapon, but found none. Desperate, she kicked him. To her surprise, he caught her foot and hauled her up to hang upside down at arm's length. She flailed and swung her fists, as he carried her from the room, but to no avail; she couldn't reach him. In her struggle, without her belt to hold it in place, her jerkin slid down, and he stopped. With a wolfish grin, he admired her small, round—if upside down—breasts.

Hilde squealed and yanked her jerkin back up. Holding it in place, she glared at him. "Filthy monster!"

The Beast chuckled, continuing on his way back down to the dungeon. As he carried her down the stairwell to the basement and the space tightened, he held Hilde closer to him. Close enough for her to strike, she knew, but without a weapon, her feeble blows would be harmless. Time was running out. If she were going to act, it would have to be quick, while still in the cramped quarters of the stairwell.

Her eyes were drawn to what she had been trying not to notice. There, not more than a foot and a half from her face, hung the huge Beast's equally proportioned genitals. Disgusted as she was by the idea, but knowing she was desperate, she seized the moment. Fast as possible,

Hilde swung her arms, lunged forward, grabbed with both hands, and squeezed.

The Beast howled in pain. He tried to throw her, but she held fast, pulling him off balance, and the two tumbled down the last few steps to land in a heap on the floor. One of her hands lost its grip in the fall, and the Beast quickly pulled himself free from the other one before straddling her and pinning her to the ground with her arms secured safely over her head.

With his face inches from hers, his heavy breathing was a hot, fetid stench. Bile rose in her throat, and she turned her head, trying not to vomit. He was in pain, and she knew it, but she was being held fast while he recovered. Her window was closing. She pulled and thrashed, but his grip was like an iron vice.

Minutes passed. Occasionally she twisted, testing his grip, but to no avail. Defiantly, she turned back to look at him and was surprised to see, for the first time, how human his eyes were. There was emotion behind them that did not belong in the eyes of a monster. She looked away, hating herself for it even as she did.

Finally, still without a word, he clasped both of her wrists with one hand and shifted his position to grab both of her ankles with his other. After flipping her up around his neck, like he had carried her before, he continued.

She saw the worry on her father's pale face when they entered but also the relief in his eyes that she was still alive.

The Beast looked at the first cell he had put her in, then to the second. After a moment's consideration, he grunted and put her down on her own two feet, keeping a tight hold on her wrists. He grabbed something off a nearby shelf and, with a little push to get her moving, he guided her back into the first cell. This time, however, he did not just push her inside and close the door. Instead, holding her wrists firmly, he directed her all the way to the back wall. Reaching down, he felt in the darkness until he found what he wanted: the chain attached to the hinged iron band. After placing the band around her neck, he affixed something to it and clicked it closed, then grunted, "*That* should hold you."

Hilde said nothing as he walked back out of the cell and slammed the door closed.

"Sit!" he demanded.

Hilde glared at the Beast before lowering herself to the floor.

The Beast smiled. "Stay!" He laughed as he turned to limp out of the dungeon. "Good girl!"

The next few days were miserable for Hilde. Being able to fit between the bars was meaningless when she could only go as far as the chain allowed. She ate twice a day when the Beast brought trays of food for her father and her. Stubborn as she was, Hilde was beginning to lose hope. She spent hours trying to free herself from the chain, and, when that didn't work, she spent hours more trying to free the chain from the wall, all to no avail. The only result was that her neck became raw and sore.

As the days passed, she and her father talked, but he continued to get sicker. His cough got worse, he stopped eating, and he grew weaker.

Hilde was desperate. Without help, he would die. "Let him go," she demanded of her captor one day when he brought their food.

"No."

"He's sick. If you don't let him go, he'll die."

The monster didn't reply at first. Then he turned for the door. "I didn't bring you here."

As he closed the door to the dungeon and left, Hilde screamed curses and made threats she knew she couldn't carry out.

The next morning, her father was much worse. He couldn't carry on a coherent conversation. He became delirious, calling out for his dead wife and sons. Hilde tried to get through to him, but nothing worked.

When the Beast arrived with that day's morning meal, in desperation, she begged. "Please! My father is very sick. If you don't let him go, he's going to die."

The Beast looked at him, then walked over to the bars for a closer look. "Mister?"

"Please! He's dying," she said, barely controlling her tears. "Just let him go."

The Beast stepped in front of her cell and looked at her. "I never invited you here. *You* came to kill me."

For a moment, she stood silently, then, having no response to his accusation, she begged. "Please!" He looked uncertain, and she pressed, "You said you'd let him go if I promised to stay. I'll stay. I won't try to kill you. I'll be your damned slave, if you want. Just, *please*, don't let him die."

"You'll stay?"

"Yes." She nodded.

"You won't leave, and you won't try to kill me."

"I swear," she agreed.

"By Odin."

Hilde nodded. "By Odin, before all the gods, I swear I will stay. I will do you no harm, and I will obey your every command."

The beast nodded, walked back to her father's cell, and unlocked the door. He lifted Erik over his shoulder and carried him from the room.

"Where are you going?" Hilde screamed. Minutes passed as she yelled and screamed, cursing him with every oath she could think of, but he didn't come back. He had taken her father and was gone. Hours dragged on as she paced back and forth in the cell, hating and vilifying him, until, at last, he returned.

"You son of a bitch," she screamed as he walked in. "Where is he? What did you do with him?" Before he could answer, she threw her plate at him. "You just took him away." The tears she had worked so hard to hold back all came pouring out now. "Where's my father?"

Eventually, when he could get a word in, the Beast explained, "I didn't know if he could make it all the way home, so I carried him as fast as I could through the woods, then watched from a distance to make certain someone found him."

Inside, Hilde felt relief and appreciated that he didn't just turn her father loose outside the castle walls to be swallowed up by the forest, but she was not about to let him know that. "You could have let me say goodbye."

For a moment, the beast stood still, uncertain what to do. He hung his head a bit, then stepped slowly forward to unlock the cell door. "I'm sorry. I just wanted to get him to some help." He unfastened the iron band from around her neck and, without another word, left the dungeon.

She felt a pang of guilt, but immediately dismissed it and chastised herself. "He's a murderous monster," she reminded herself. "And I am still a prisoner."

Leaving the dungeon, she wasn't quite sure what to do. She'd sworn to stay, so she would, but what was she to do alone with a monster in the near ruins of this old castle? Smelling herself after days in a dingy cage, the idea of fresh air and sunlight encouraged her to make her way outside.

"Girl," the Beast called as she entered the Grand Foyer.

"Girl?" she snapped. "I have a name, Beast."

Anger flared in his eyes, but then he closed them and calmed down. Opening them, he nodded. "My apologies. I do not know your name."

She considered him for a moment. "Hilde. My name is Hilde Eriksdotter."

He inclined his head in acknowledgment. "And I am Thor. Prince Thor Bjornson."

"Only men need names, Beast, and you are no man."

Rage filled his eyes, and, for a moment, she feared he might kill her, but the air around the room took on the slightest of pink hues, and he silently collected himself. The pink illumination flowed through the windows from the courtyard outside.

"I only wanted to tell you," he spoke through gritted teeth, "that the North Wing upstairs is off limits. You may wander anywhere but there."

Hilde smiled to herself and started for the door, satisfied that she would hold to her oath, but nothing more. She would stay, but he would not enjoy her presence.

Outside, it was cold, but the evening sunlight felt pleasant, and the crisp, clean air was both refreshing and invigorating. Shivering, she wrapped her arms around herself and listened to the birds sing. She walked around the courtyard admiring the beautiful pink rosebushes, awed by their beauty in the dead of winter. She brushed a velvet petal and sniffed its sweet aroma. At her gentle touch, the rosebush seemed to chime like many little bells, making her smile in wonder.

The castle door closed, drawing her attention, and she turned to face the Beast, only to find that he was not there. Instead, on the steps lay her fur-lined cloak, which she had cast off in the dungeon before their first battle. She looked around suspiciously, but he was gone.

Retrieving the warm, heavy cloak and wrapping it around her shoulders, she felt a sense of gratitude but immediately cursed him for tricking her. The whole episode had soured her mood, and, as she wandered around the castle's grounds, she wondered what game the Beast was playing. Why hadn't he just killed her and her father as soon as they arrived? Why had he let her father go on only her promise to remain? And why, after she had tried so hard to kill him, was he being so nice to her? He was up to something, but what?

So many questions twisted and turned in her mind that she lost track of time, and, as the sun set and the woods grew dark, she heard unnatural sounds that jarred her from her thoughts. The woods seemed to emanate a sense of foreboding. It felt frigid all of a sudden. Pulling her cloak a little tighter, she stepped quickly back into the castle.

The Grand Foyer was dark when she entered, dark and cold. Her stomach rumbled, reminding her how long it had been since she last ate. Able to make out only the barest outlines in the blackness, Hilde felt her way back to the kitchen where the beast had lit a fire and was roasting a rabbit while he ate a raw one himself. The sight was disgusting, so she focused on the roasting rabbit and thenclosed her eyes. The smell was delicious, and she tried to block out the sounds of his low growling, chomping, and lip smacking.

"Where am I to sleep?" she asked, quickly losing her appetite.

"I don't care," he said, around a mouthful of meat. "Pick any room you like."

"And where am I to bathe?"

"There are tubs around here. I'll find one tomorrow and put it wherever you want." He spat out a bone. "Then you can draw water from the well." He shrugged. "Heat it over the fire in your room."

Hilde reluctantly opened her eyes and started glancing around. She stood in a necropolis, surrounded by the remains of countless animals, picked clean and cast aside. The stench of death lay heavy in the air.

"What do you need?" the Beast asked, wiping his snout.

"Something to use as a torch. I can't see in the dark."

He walked across the kitchen and returned a moment later with a torch in hand. "It's old," he shrugged, "but I think it should still work."

Taking the torch, Hilde looked at it, then put it to the flames under her roasting rabbit. "I'll be back in a few minutes," she informed him, seeing that her meal was not yet done. "I'm just going to pick a room." And get away from you, she thought but kept that last part to herself.

The beast said nothing, but she could feel his eyes on her as she walked out of the room. Wandering the halls at night, with only a torch's light, was very intimidating. The broken wreckage of furniture and the shadows the torchlight spread across the walls created a sinister atmosphere. Still wrapped in her warm cloak, she shivered.

After making her way back to the Grand Foyer, she walked up the stairs to the second floor, where she expected the bedrooms to be. Instead of turning right, toward the room with the pink rose from which she was now forbidden, she turned left. As expected, some of the doors were swollen shut, and others opened to reveal a broken mess. As she surveyed the damage, she suspected they had been destroyed in some sort of feral rage.

At last, she shouldered open a stuck door to reveal a spacious comfortable sitting room. Time and neglect had left their mark; moths and mice had chewed the linens and drapes, but this room appeared to have escaped its master's fury. A bedroom, she found, lay through a door to the left, a balcony on the south wall of the castle was across from the hallway door, and, through a door in the bedroom, she discovered a bathing and powder room. The sitting room alone was bigger than their cottage back home, and, although it was in a state of disrepair, Hilde felt a sense of excitement about her new suite. Though she intended to make the Beast miserable, there was no reason for her to be.

Her stomach rumbled, reminding her that she still hadn't eaten. So, having made her decision, she headed back to the kitchen. The rooms she had chosen were not only in comparatively good condition but were also about as far from the Beast's Pink Room as she could get.

When she returned, the kitchen was empty. The Beast had taken the roast rabbit off the fire and laid it on the table before banking the coals and leaving. She was glad he was gone. Just thinking about trying to eat with his crunching and smacking turned her stomach. Taking her meal from his graveyard of a kitchen to the Banquet Hall, she placed the torch in a wall sconce. The immense table had been shoved against the wall but was undamaged. After setting aright an overturned unbroken chair, she sat down to eat. The rabbit, she found, was not well-cooked, and she was forced to return to the kitchen and lay it low over the hot coals, ignoring the sights and smells around her. When it was finally cooked to her liking, Hilde returned to her seat at the massive, dusty Banquet Hall table. The meat was delicious.

After she had eaten her fill and wrapped up the leftover rabbit, Hilde took the torch and food and headed off to her new quarters. She put the rabbit meat by the balcony door where it was coldest, or at least would be if there were a fire in the fireplace and the room weren't freezing. After pulling the top blanket off the bed gently, so as not to stir up the thick layer of dust covering it, she used the torch to look more closely at the other blankets. Satisfied that they were usable, she pulled them off the bed and curled up on the floor. After all these years, anything could have nested in that mattress, and she was not about to get eaten during the night.

Even with the blankets, the night was still cold, but today had been exhausting, and sleep found her quickly

In the morning, Hilde woke as dawn's fingers stretched long across the room that she could now see, in the light of day, was even better than she had expected. It had been abandoned and neglected, but not destroyed like so many of the other rooms. The windows were all intact, and, aside from the moth and rodent damage and the thick coat of dust, it was in reasonably good shape. There was so much dust, in fact, that last night's steps had left footprints like in a dusting of snow.

After a simple but satisfying breakfast of cold rabbit meat, Hilde threw open all the room's doors and windows and set to work. If she were going to live here, it would be clean. She drew water from the well and found cleaning supplies: a broom, dustpan, mop, and duster in a closet down the hall. It took all day, but when she'd finished, her new rooms were spotless, there was wood stacked by the fireplace—which she had gathered and split herself—and a big kettle of water heated over the fire for her first bath since leaving home. Buckets of fresh water lined the wall on the other side of the fireplace. While she was working, the Beast had brought a tub and placed it where she directed.

A search of the nearest rooms' closets produced an assortment of clothing, most of which were moth eaten, but many were still salvageable, and some appeared untouched. A large portion of those were gaudy court dress, but she was able to find a few outfits she could wear, after washing them, of course.

Back in her room, she filled her tub, undressed and slowly lowered herself into the hot steaming water. The effect was instantaneous, and, as she lay back in the tub, the stress melted away. She closed her eyes and relaxed for a while, then, when she was ready, bathed with fine expensive soaps.

The fire had warmed the room sufficiently so that, after she had bathed and emptied the water out the window, she knelt beside the refilled tub and washed the clothes she had been wearing and some of those she had salvaged. After rinsing them in hot clean water, they were wrung out as best she could and hung up around her rooms to dry. Throughout the week, she would wash the rest, followed by an assortment of linens.

She had been able to find a mattress that was undamaged and appeared to contain no unwanted guests. It had been quite a struggle to drag it to her room, but she knew that it would be well worth the effort. Tonight, for the first time in her life, she would sleep on the plush comfort of a feather mattress.

The sun had set, but she now had a small stack of torches to light her room, and, wrapped in a thin robe that had dried quickly after the wash, she gazed into the fire and nibbled on the last of the rabbit meat from the night before. Busy with her cleaning, Hilde had not seen the Beast all day. That was fine with her, but she wondered why he had wanted her to stay. At first, she assumed he wanted company, but, so far, since releasing her from the dungeon, she had seen little of him, and he had never sought her out.

A few days passed, and she still saw very little of him. He hunted and provided her with meat but rarely spoke more than necessary. One day, however, while she was still in the kitchen cooking soup with his meat and roots she had dug up herself, he appeared in the doorway and just stood there watching her cook.

"You need something?" she asked.

He shrugged. "Not really. It's just been a long time since I smelled real cooking."

Again, silence stretched for a few minutes before he asked, "So why exactly did you come here?"

"To kill you," she answered matter-of-factly.

He smiled and nodded. "Yes. I understand that, but why? Why now?"

For a moment, she said nothing as she stirred her soup. At last, she replied, "Because you murdered two of my brothers."

He nodded sadly. "I don't like killing men."

She glared at him but said nothing.

"I'm sorry for your loss, but they shouldn't have come hunting me."

"They weren't hunting you," she spat angrily. "They were coming home after celebrating the winter solstice with my mother's kin."

"Then why did they come here?"

She looked at him as if he were daft. "They didn't come here, you monster. They were part of the caravan you slaughtered two and a half weeks ago.

Shaking his head, he denied it. "I've never attacked anyone. I certainly did not attack any caravan."

"Don't bullshit me, Beast. I was there. I saw with my own eyes the carnage you left on the road."

"Road? Except for returning your father, I haven't been anywhere near a road in years."

"Liar!" Hilde screamed, hurling a spoon at his head.

The Beast easily ducked the projectile.

"You're a monster!" she spat. "A hateful monster who killed my brothers."

Realizing that there would be no reasoning with her, the Beast turned and left the room.

It wasn't until the next day that she saw him again. She was in the courtyard, pruning the rosebushes when the Beast came out of the woods with a deer slung around his neck. He stopped and for a moment, just watched her. When it was obvious that she was ignoring him, he said, "I know I look like a monster, but inside I'm still a man."

Hilde laughed scornfully. "You're a monster through and through; there's nothing human about you. You're an animal."

"I'm not."

Looking up, she sneered at him. "Men bathe; men wear clothes; men cook their food and eat at tables." Her voice rose with her fury and disgust. "Men don't leave their kills in their houses to putrefy and rot." Her volume dropped as her eyes narrowed. "You may walk upright like a man and talk like a man, but you're no man."

Without any response, the Beast shifted the burden on his shoulder and shuffledinto the castle.

She didn't see him again until the next morning. After her normal routine of washing her face, dressing, and brushing her hair, Hilde left her room to find the Beast coming up the stairs. At the sight of him, she burst out laughing. He was dressed in patchwork pants and jacket.

His eyes dropped to the floor, and he shifted uncomfortably. "I was just coming to invite you to breakfast."

"Invite me to breakfast?" she scoffed. "Shall I sit and watch as you slobber over bite after bloody bite?"

"I …" he shifted nervously and tried again. "I cooked us a meal of meat and gravy made with the last of the rice flour from storage. I tried to make biscuits too, but it didn't work out."

Just then, the aroma wafted up, and she had to admit it smelled delicious. For several days, she'd eaten nothing but venison and rabbit. A pot of gravy sounded delicious.

The moment of weakness was brief, however. Another glance at him strengthened her resolve. "I'll eat by myself."

His shoulders hunched, and his lips drew back menacingly. Gone was the uncertainty. Now he exuded pure confidence. "You will eat ..."

The pink rose in his lapel blazed, cutting his words short. After taking a moment to calm himself, he tried again. "Please do me the honor of dining with me."

It had required an act of will to hold her ground and not step back in the face of his momentary rage. Now thinking it wise simply to accept the invitation, she nodded and followed him down the stairs. Besides, this show might well prove entertaining.

Had he slept at all last night? she wondered. The Grand Foyer and the kitchen were clean, the remnants of past meals and broken furniture were gone, and it appeared that he had made an attempt at sweeping. Even the Banquet Hall was clean, or at least relatively clean. The windows had been washed—if poorly—so that the morning light now lit the room brightly. The table was covered with a moth-eaten but clean white cloth and, compared to her recent meals, a feast.

A glow from the rose reminded the Beast of his court etiquette, and he held the chair for Hilde to sit before seating himself at the head of the table.

Hilde was more amused than anything by this display: a monster playing at being a man. As he fumbled with the serving utensils, she smirked. "What happened to your finger?" she asked, seeing that one of his big meaty forefingers was hurt.

"My experience with a needle and thread is limited," he explained with a forced smile.

She laughed out loud. "You did that to your finger while sewing?"

His whole body stiffened, and the wooden spoon in his hand split in two, but another flaring of his lapel rose calmed his temper, and he took a moment to regain control before serving. "I've lived out here alone for so long that clothes seemed unnecessary. But now that I have a guest ..."

"Prisoner," she immediately corrected.

"Now that I have company," he compromised, "I want to ..." He hesitated, looking for the right word.

She didn't give him the chance. "Listen, Beast. You can play dress up, you can cook food and eat at a table, but you're still just a monster pretending to be human. A horrible murderous monster."

Again, he stiffened in anger, and again the flower flared. Silence passed between them for a moment as she questioned her own wisdom at poking an angry bear. Or a wolf, in this case. He slumped into his chair and sighed. "I bathed too."

A snide comment came to mind as she envisioned him licking his fur, but she checked herself. After a moment, with the food still untouched on their plates, she asked, "Why do you want me here, and why are you trying to be something you're clearly not?"

"I want you here because I've been alone for a long, long time, and I'm terribly lonely." He looked at her, pleading for understanding. "And I'm not pretending to be something I'm not. Despite my current form, I am a man, a prince in fact. It's just been a long time since I had cause to act like one."

For the first time, she actually felt sympathy for this creature beside her. Immediately the images of her brothers' torn bodies strengthened her resolve and hatred. "If that is true," she glared at him, "then you are worse than I ever imagined."

"I …" he began, but she cut him off.

"An animal does harm not out of malice, but because it's in its nature. If you are indeed, as you claim, a man in that bestial form, then you understand the harm you do and are doubly guilty."

"What harm?" he asked, raising his voice and fighting to quiet it. "I live alone in this castle in the middle of this accursed woods. I've never hurt anyone who didn't come here looking to kill me."

"You murdered my brothers in a caravan on the East Road!" she screamed.

Unable to control himself, the Beast shot to his feet. "I did not!"

Standing up as tall as she could, Hilde stood her ground and glared at him. In a menacing whisper, she said, "I saw the bodies, Beast. I saw the four clean slashes that opened Haaken's belly, so his guts spilled out. Nothing else," she continued, her voice rising as her eyes took on a murderous rage, "not man nor beast can make such marks as those."

In a soft voice and with his claws raised, he asked, "Do I make such marks as those you describe?" Stepping around the table, the Beast laid his hand on it, pressed his claws into it, and slowly approached her, gouging the tabletop. "You've seen the marks my claws make; they don't slice, they tear."

When he stopped before her, she stared in silence at him and at the rough, uneven marks he had made.

"You said that neither man nor beast makes marks like these, so think about what you've seen. Have you ever seen a man killed in the manner in which I kill?" He walked around her, circling back toward his own seat.

Hilde opened her mouth to argue but closed it again. After a moment, considering what she had seen and what she knew, she dropped into her chair. She watched him sit too, but her mind was a jumble of confusion and uncertainty.

"I did not kill your brothers," the Beast repeated. "These woods were not only intended to keep people out, but also to keep me in. The deeper into the woods I go, the more turned around I get. It's very difficult for me to reach the villages or roads. Taking your father home was the first time I've been near a village or road in many years."

Hilde did not want to believe him, wanted to scream at him that he was a liar and a murderer. But he was right. She had seen the wounds inflicted by his claws on the animals he had brought in for food. She had seen the raked and torn flesh, and it was nothing like the marks on her brothers' dead bodies. She wanted him to be guilty, but, as she thought it over, the Beast was incapable of making those wounds.

"Then someone tried to make it look like you had done it," she admitted reluctantly.

He nodded. "Someone played on people's fear of me to get away with murder."

After a moment, she said, "You have to let me go then to find out who it was and to avenge my brothers' deaths.

"You swore."

"I know, but ..."

"You swore," he repeated.

114

"Yes, I swore," she agreed, leaning back in her chair. "I gave my word, and I'll keep it."

"If you remain here until the next winter's solstice," he said gently and closed his eyes, "the day after solstice, your oath will be fulfilled."

She nodded, and, for the first time since arriving, offered a hesitant smile. "Thank you."

In response, he offered what she thought passed for a weak smile of his own before picking up a fork in his oversized hand. "Now please, try to eat your food."

Again, she smiled, a genuine smile. She felt a great sense of lightness, of ease, as if a great weight had been lifted off her shoulders. The hatred she had been clinging to so desperately evaporated with the knowledge that this creature had not killed her brothers. She wasn't quite certain how to feel about him, but now he was cast in a new light.

"This is really very good," she said, looking up after a few bites, at which time she saw him shovel spoonful after spoonful into his mouth.

A glow of the rose in his lapel drew his attention, and he slowed down. Hilde turned back to her gravy and shrugged.

As she ate, she turned to a more serious topic. "You said that you have killed men who came hunting you."

The smile vanished. "I had no choice. They would have killed me."

She nodded. "So why didn't you kill me?"

A smile crept across his face, and he shrugged.

"Do you think I'm so easy to beat that you weren't in any real danger?"

His eyes went wide. "Oh no! You did me far more injury than any of them did."

"Then why?"

Looking back at his meal, he shrugged again. She was about to press him when he answered, "You were too pretty."

"Pretty?"

He looked at her again. "I haven't seen a beautiful girl in a very long time. I knew what I was risking, but I just couldn't kill someone as beautiful as you. You were like a warrior princess or a Valkyrie."

"A Valkyrie," she repeated and grinned.

Looking down, he stared at his plate.

Hilde laughed. "What did you say your name is?"

He looked up, surprised. "Thor," he smiled. "Prince Thor Bjornson."

"Well, Thor, I'm honored to be compared to a Valkyrie."

They ate in silence for a few minutes before Hilde asked, "So, I kind of get why you let me live, but why didn't you kill my father? He's a stalwart warrior, and he would have killed you if given half a chance."

"I don't like killing. I hunt, of course, but killing men is different. Your father was exhausted after struggling through the woods. He was not at his best. Had he been thinking, he would have rested before coming after me, but he was driven by something other than reason. He was pushed on by hate. He pushed himself beyond exhaustion and was in no condition to wage battle. He was also bespelled by the rosebush."

"But still," she said, "he came to kill you. What did you intend to do with him?"

He shrugged. "I guess I hadn't decided." He smiled. "But then, when I saw you, I could never have hurt him."

When breakfast was over, Hilde volunteered to wash the dishes, which provided her with an opportunity to consider this revelation. She had heard the stories, since birth, of the prince who had offended the gods and, for his wickedness, had been transformed into a mindless Beast with an insatiable bloodlust. The truth, it now seemed, was very different. Clearly, he had been transformed, but Thor was no mindless beast, and, from what she could tell, he was not driven by a lust for blood. She wondered what he could have done to offend the gods that they would change him into a monster.

As she was finishing the dishes, a loud crash drew her attention, and she ran to the Grand Foyer, then jumped back as large pieces of broken furniture came raining down from above.

"What are you doing?"

Thor's head popped up over the railing, and he grinned. "Spring cleaning?"

She laughed. "It's winter."

His grin softened into a gentle smile. "You've reminded me of what it is to be a man; I no longer want to live amongst the trash like an animal." He looked around at the walls and ceilings. "I'm going to return this castle to its former glory. It was beautiful, you know."

Trying to imagine it in its heyday, she smiled. "I'm sure it was."

Over the next few weeks, they worked and enjoyed light conversation. Questions nagged at her, pleading to be asked, but she kept them to herself. As she washed windows, a task to which her small hands were much better suited, she watched Thor lift and carry things that would have required a few big men. To her surprise, she began to see him in a whole new light. Where before, she could only see the fur, snout, and claws, she now began to see beauty and grace in his form. He was so powerful, but also so gentle. His huge hands were clumsy, but he took such care.

One day, as winter released its icy grip, and the ground and trees began to sprout green, Hilde cut her foot on a piece of broken glass. Thor, so large and imposing, lifted her into his arms and carried her to the kitchen where he cleaned and wrapped her injury with a soft touch of such tenderness that she would not have believed him capable.

A few weeks later, while he was doing repairs, he accidentally knocked loose a bird's nest and found baby birds too small to fly; he gently plucked them from the floor and carried them to the kitchen. Their mother never returned, but he lovingly cared for and tended to those little birds. Hilde helped, but there was little for her to do; his devotion to the small helpless creatures was complete. In time, she even stopped noticing his bestial form. Thor was a kind and gentle person. Even after all these years of solitude and barbarity, it was like flipping a switch, and the educated and cultured prince had returned.

Life returned to the castle's environs. Fruit took shape on the trees, flowers grew, andcreatures began to scurry across the lush green grass. Together Hilde and Thor walked the grounds, talked, and gardened, making their prison into a haven. One bright spring morning, Thor brought to the garden the two baby birds he had so lovingly raised. In his massive hands, he lifted both birds from their cage. "Goodbye, little ones," he whispered through the cracks between his fingers. "You can always come back now and then. You'll always have a home here."

When he looked up, Hilde, surprised to see that a wolf could cry, saw tears glistening at the corners of his eyes. She smiled at him and nodded, and he opened his hands, gently tossing his two charges up into the air, and, after a few unsuccessful tries, they took wing and flew away. Watching them disappear over the castle wall, she took Thor's hand in both of hers and offered it a reassuring squeeze. "They'll be fine now."

Tearing his gaze from the sky, he nodded at her with a sad smile. "They say that if you love something, you have to let it go, and if it loves you, it will come back." He looked up again at where they had disappeared, "Maybe they'll come back."

One day, after watching Hilde struggle to pull down one of the thick vines that grew up and threatened to smother the castle, Thor came over and, with a tug, yanked it free. Coming more easily than he expected, it sent Hilde and him backward to the ground. They laughed together for a moment, then Hilde got up on her knees and turned to face him.

"At least you fell on something big and furry," Thor laughed.

She smiled. "You're not exactly soft, you know.

Propping himself on one arm, he brushed his fingers down her cheek. Caught off-guard, she didn't move, just smiled at his gentle touch. As quickly as the moment came, it passed.He withdrew his hand, and she stood up, then offered her hand to help him up.

Uncertain what to do, Hilde hadallowed this show of his affection and thentried to sort out her feelings. As they continued working, she watched him, unable to deny what she felt for him but also scaredof feeling it. Then again, what exactly was it that she did feel for him? That was the problem; she didn't know.

Spring turned to summer, and the castle was in as good shape as was possible without supplies to replace broken windows or other specialized repairs. Hilde, very wellpracticed with a needle and thread, surprised Thor with two sets of clothes made out of the undamaged parts of moth-eaten curtains, sheets, and other large pieces of material.

"You made these for me?" he asked, amazed by the gesture.

Smiling, she reached out and tugged on one of the seams of his poorly made pants, which promptly split again. "You're good at a lot of things, Thor, but sewing isn't one of them."

"Don't I know it!" He pointed toother tears in his clothes. "Every night I have to sew up a new hole." Turning to her with sincere gratitude, he smiled. "Thank you."

"You're welcome. Now go try them on."

"They're perfect," he said when he came back a few minutes later.

Hilde looked him over with a critical eye, then nodded. "Yeah, that's actually a pretty good fit." She patted his chest. "Next, I'm going to make you a dinner jacket. I just have to find the right material, and I've looked everywhere."

"Use anything you want," he offered, admiring the sleeves and cuffs of his new shirt.

Smiling, she bounded off to look around some more. After searching everywhere she could think of without success, she found herself at the top of the staircase, looking down the north hall toward the Pink Room. That was some sort of private sanctuary, she knew, and when she had agreed to stay, she hadpromised not to go in there, but there were other rooms on either side of the hall that she had never been in. As long as she didn't go into that room, she decided, it would probably be okay.

Some of the doors were stuck and required some effort to open, but inside she discovered a trove of useful items. The fifth room she entered was dark; curtains had been left drawn against the bright day. Opening them, she found that the outer curtains were fragile and useless after so long in the bright sun, but the inner curtains were of exquisite blue velvet. Excited, she climbed on a nearby chair to unhook them from the rod on which they hung.

In the now brightly lit room, she examined the velvet, certain that it was perfect for Thor's new dinner jacket. After folding it up neatly, she turned to leave and froze. Before she could stop it, a scream erupted from her throat, a scream born of the deepest terror. There, before her, was something from a nightmare. In the large plush bed lay the stone figure of a woman contorted into an unnatural and horrific position, her mouth open and twisted in a silent scream. Unable to think, she could only stare, frozen in place by the gruesome scene.

More time passed before movement caught her eye. Her head spun to find Thor's massive bulk in the doorway. Her feet took an unconscious step back.

"I told you to stay out of the north wing," he said. His voice held no anger, only pity.

It took a moment before Hilde found her voice. "What is that?"

A tear trickled down the big monster's face. "I haven't been in this room since the day it happened."

"Happened? Was that a real person?" she asked, knowing the answer before she asked.

He nodded, his eyes riveted on the horrific petrifaction.

"Who was she?"

"I never knew her name. She was just one of Halya's ladies-in-waiting."

"Halya?" she asked, unfamiliar with the name.

Turning to look at Hilde, Thor asked in surprise, "Don't you know what happened here?"

She had wondered, had even considered asking, but now she questioned whether she even wanted to know. Despite herself, she shook her head. "I only know you committed a crime so offensive that the gods cursed you."

A weak sardonic smile crossed his lips. "Is that what people believe? That I offended the gods?"

She hesitated, uncertain, then nodded.

"How did I offend them?" he asked, curious.

Looking back and forth between him and the bed, she said, "I've heard different things, but the most common is that you," she hesitated, then, firming her resolve, she continued, "you murdered your betrothed." She watched him for any clues but saw none. "Is ... Is that her?"

"No," he answered simply.

"Did you kill your betrothed?"

Thor turned to the window, remembering that fateful morning, but he said nothing. Seconds ticked by in silence before he finally said, "Yes, but not in the way you mean."

"I don't understand."

Turning back to her, his voice was barely a whisper. "My father died, and I was to be crowned king, but to take the throne, I first had to be married."

Hilde listened in silence.

"My father had already chosen a wife for me before he died. A beautiful girl of royal line. She had been orphaned as a child and was raised by Olga, high priestess of the goddess Freyja. The ceremony was the event of the century, and we were wed with a great celebration. It was a wonderful day. That night, we were, of course, to consummate our union. I was very eager, but my young wife was scared. Certain that we would have many nights together, I simply held her, and she fell asleep in my arms.

"In the morning, after she had gone to prepare for our coronation, one of her ladies remained behind, and, within seconds of my new wife leaving, this lady and I were rolling around on my wedding bed. "I don't know if she forgot something or ... I just don't know, maybe she just wanted to see me, but for some reason, Halya returned. She found us in bed together. I don't know what came over her. I've been over it a thousand times, and I can't understand it. She ran over to the window, that one," he said, pointing, "and threw herself out. When I got to the window, she was dead on the stones below."

"But I don't understand," Hilde said, then she paused. "How did ..."

He held up a hand, and, when she fell silent, he continued. "Almost immediately, Olga rushed in. She ran to the window, and, seeing Halya's body below, spun on me and on the girl still on my bed. Olga cast magic and as I watched, the girl in the bed was slowly, painfully turned into stone.

"I was terrified, certain I was to share the same fate, but Olga couldn't kill me because of an oath she had sworn. Instead, she did far worse. She cursed me and turned me into this monster. I passed out from the pain of the transformation, so I don't know what happened next. I only know that when I woke, my mother was dying, and my own guards were trying to kill me. Everyone fled, and the dark woods grew up around my castle. I've been a prisoner ever since."

The room was quiet for a few moments before Hilde, looking at the window, whispered, "So you didn't kill her."

"Not directly, but my actions led to her death. I am responsible."

She walked over and took his huge hand in hers. "You're not responsible," she told him, looking up into his eyes.

He looked away.

"Thor," she spoke, gently turning his face back to hers. "You didn't kill her." She stroked the soft fur on his cheek. "She is responsible for her own actions; she jumped, and the gods will hold her accountable. Odin will not hold you guilty for her death." She gently guided him out of the room and pulled the door closed.

"But if I ..."

"Stop!" The tone of her voice silenced him, and, when he looked at her, she said, "Guilt is a burden that is easy to pick up, heavy to carry, and hard to put down. We gather enough of it on our own; we don't need to pick up other people's too."

Smiling softly at her, he asked, "What made you so wise?"

Sadness filled her eyes. "You are not the only one who has known loss or who has picked up that burden for himself."

His big furry arms gently enveloped her, and in their warmth and security, she did something she rarely did: she wept. A moment later, he carried her out into the courtyard, into the bright, warm sun. In the protection of his arms, she knew she was safe, and, when she was in control of herself again, although he hadn't asked, she felt compelled to explain.

"My father had gone hunting. He had taken Leif and Haakon. I was left in charge to watch my younger brother Harold and my little sister Ilse."

As Thor sat down against the warm stone wall, Hilde snuggled close. "I saw the two of them go out to play, but I was busy with needlework, and I left them to it." She tried to swallow the lump in her throat. "When they didn't come home, I went looking for them. I searched for hours." As the memories flowed from her heart, tears flowed down her cheeks. "They had been playing by the river, and Ilse had fallen into the water. Harold, the brave little fool," she smiled through her tears, "jumped in to save her. They were swept downriver. Harold reached Ilse and wouldn't let go. Holding her, he caught a branch on a tree that leaned far out over the river.

"So young and yet so strong, he held her for hours. If only he had let her go, he could have climbed out of the river, but he didn't. Ilya eventually heard his screams and pulled them both from the river. He brought them home, and I did all I could to warm them and ..." She choked on her sobs. "I tried, but I couldn't save them."

"Shh," he hushed her, rocking her back and forth. "That wasn't your fault," he whispered. "It was just an accident, a tragic accident."

Hilde fought for control, struggled to stop the spasms that wracked her body. It took time and effort, but, at last, she regained her composure enough to speak. "I know it wasn't my fault. I can blame myself by saying that I shouldn't have let them play outside, but they always played outside, just like I did at their age. I could blame myself, but nothing good would come of it, so I accept that it's not my fault." She looked up into his soft brown eyes. "Just like Halya's death was not your fault."

Offering her a weak smile, he nodded.

One sunny summer day, less than two weeks before the solstice, while the days were warm and bright and life around the castle was plentiful and vibrant, Thor returned from a hunt. "Hilde," he shouted, dropping his deer on the kitchen worktable.

She appeared a moment later. "Thor?" she asked, "What's wrong?"

"Men move in the woods."

She looked at him curiously. "What?"

"When I was hunting, I heard noises, noises that were unnatural to the woods," he explained. "When I investigated, I saw men, two dozen or so, trying to navigate the woods." He hesitated for a moment, but, before she could question him, he added. "Hilde, they were led by your father."

She turned to the window, "Father?" then back to Thor. "He's coming here?"

"He's trying to, but the woods are fighting back.

"I remember."

"It's hard for one person, but almost impossible for groups of men," he explained. "The vines are larger and more numerous; the muddy sinkholes that open under your feet become big enough to swallow an army; the disorientation makes anyone lost, turning in different directions. I've never seen more than two get through at once. If they don't turn around, they're doomed."

She stared at him, hanging on his every word, her lip trembling as tears threatened to overcome her. "You've got to save them."

"There's only one way I can save them." He stepped close and wrapped his arms around her. "I love you, Hilde," he whispered. "I want you to stay here with me forever. I can't stand the thought of losing you, but I also can't let them die."

"What?"

"The only way to save them is to turn them around, and the only way they'll do that is if you go to them." Tears poured from his eyes as he opened his embrace. "Go, Hilde. Go and save them. I release you from your oath."

For a moment, she stood still, desperate to go to them yet also desperate to stay with him.

"GO!" he roared.

Startled, she flinched. "Thank you," she yelled and ran for the door.

Having grabbed neither her leather jerkin nor her axe, with only her knife belted to her hip over a pretty white dress, Hilde plunged into the trees. Her only thought was to turn her father and his hunting party around before the woods swallowed them whole. Branches whipped at her face, and roots tripped up her feet, but she paid no mind as she ran. Heading out, the woods wasn't fighting her; only the natural obstacles stood in her way as she plowed desperately through the underbrush.

Without the woods' hindrances, she made good time and soon heard men shouting. Out of breath and tripping over her skirt, she ran toward the noise and found the group of men hacking at vines that were wrapping around their feet. Scanning the men's faces, she finally found the one she was seeking.

"Father!" she screamed as loudly as she could to be heard above the din. "Father!"

"Hilde!" He stared as she ran toward him, and he caught her in his arms. "My baby! You're alive!"

She held him, squeezing him desperately, overwhelmed with emotion at feeling his strong, loving arms around her. A few moments passed before she recognized the chaos about her. "Turn around," she shouted to be heard by everyone. "Going deeper is suicide. We must turn around."

"Not while it lives!" Ilya shouted. "I'm gonna kill it or die trying."

The rest of the men took up Ilya's shout, and Hilde knew then that this wasn't just a rescue mission. "What happened?" she asked her father.

"He slaughtered another caravan. Ilya's youngest, little Bridget, was only four."

"He didn't do it!"

Her father turned to look at her as if she were daft. "Oh, he did it."

"When, Father? When did this happen?"

"Two days ago."

"Two days ago, Thor was with me. In the morning we picked the rest of the food from the garden, then we spent the afternoon together in the courtyard. He didn't do this."

"The slashes on their bodies ..." he began, but she cut him off.

"His claws don't slash like knives, Father. They tear like any other claws. Trust me," she pleaded. "He didn't do this."

Seeing his skepticism and hoping she was getting through to him, she went on. "Thor didn't kill Leif or Haakon or any of them. He's not like that."

"Erik," Ilya shouted, hacking at the growing vines. "That monster has bewitched her. We need to end this." A vine got hold of his ankle and dragged him. He yelled, swinging wildly and cutting the vine. Regaining his feet, he growled. "The curse will die with him. We must kill the monster."

"Please, Father," Hilde pleaded but knew it was in vain. That stubborn hardness passed over his face, his eyes turning to cold steel.

"Go home, Hilde," he told her, starting forward and swinging at an incoming vine. "We have to see this through."

"How do you think you got home? How did you get home from his castle?"

He stopped. "What?"

"Thor carried you, Father. He carried you out through these woods and brought you home safely. He isn't a killer." Grabbing his arm, Hilde fell to her knees. "Please stop!"

Defending themselves against the vines, the small army had been separated into three smaller groups. As Erik pulled himself away from her grasp, havoc erupted as the ground under Ilya's group turned soft. The men yelled and struggled to pull themselves out of the thick mud and onto dry ground, but the harder they fought, the faster they sank.

Hilde watched as her father ran toward the mud, toward his friends. Ilya, always a fighter, was sinking fast. "Grab this," Erik yelled, throwing out a long vine that had just been hacked off. When Ilya had a good hold, Erik pulled. His muscles bulged with the effort as he pulled with every ounce of strength he could muster. Hilde caught hold of the vine then, and other men joined, but all their efforts only prevented his sinking any further. They could not overcome the suction of the mud.

Efforts had been made to save the other two caught in the mud with Ilya, but his was now the only head above the surface. As more and more men hauled at the vine, the soft ground began to expand, threatening to swallow all of them.

"Heave!" Erik yelled, and the line of men on the vine pulled in unison. They gained a step backward, but all their efforts made insignificant progress for Ilya.

Struggling to keep his head above the surface, Ilya looked at Erik. "Not the noble death in battle that I imagined."

"We'll get you out," Erik yelled, lifting his foremost foot out of the sinking ground.

"No, old friend. Odin calls my name."

"No!" Erik cried. "Heave!" Again, as one, the men pulled and tumbled back in a heap as their burden released his grip.

"No!"

"Avenge me," Ilya called out as he sank beneath the surface.

Immediately, Hilde grabbed her father to restrain him from going to his friend and his death. "He's gone," she said, softly but firmly. "Now we must turn around, or these woods will kill each and every one of us.

"I must avenge him."

"You cannot avenge him against the very ground we stand on," she insisted, forcing his face around to hers. "To proceed will be to throw away the lives of every one of these brave men. How will the gods look upon you for that? How willyou be judged?"

Looking around at all the faces that watched Erik and awaited his decision, she knew they wouldhave followed if he had gone on. Even knowing certain death lay ahead, they wouldhave followed. She heard him take a deep breath to steady himself. "We cannot avenge our fallen brothers if we die today." She saw a mixture of emotions: some relief and some disappointment. "We aren't giving up," he assured them forcefully. "We're regrouping and rethinking our plan. We *will* have our revenge!"

As Hilde and her father started back toward their village, the other men fell in behind, and the woods allowed them safe passage back out.

Back home, Hilde could find no peace. Everyone wanted stories about the Beast and what horrors she had endured at his evil hands. At first, she tried to explain to them about Thor but soon gave up. They didn't want to hear the truth. They wanted their monster. She must have been bespelled, they said, magically tricked and brainwashed by the evil Beast.

By most, she was looked on with either pity for all the horrors she must have endured, or disgust for her weakness in allowing the monster to corrupt her mind and who knew what else. Most of the young men, who used to show off and fight to impress her, now avoided her, while the girls ostracized her, staring and falling silent whenever she approached.

For the first few weeks, she threw herself into her training as a shield maiden, a warrior woman. Others came to the clearing to fight and train but then left. Hilde trained to exhaustion, resting only long enough to muster her strength before resuming her exercise.

"Pretty good, for a girl."

Hilde spun and glared at the newcomer, then softened. "Sigurd," she hesitated, "I'm so sorry about your father."

A shadow of sorrow passed across his face, but then he smiled. His eyes, those soft brown depths, looked so much like Ilya's. The rest of him, however, was all from his mother's side: tall and lean. He was broad of chest and narrow of waist, and his arms were tightly corded muscle, ending in bony fists, one of which now tightened around the handle of wooden practice sword. "I have no doubt that he has his seat at Odin's table."

"No doubt," she agreed. "Ilya was like a second father to me." She fought the tears that threatened to overcome her. "I loved him very much."

Sigurd nodded. "And he loved you. That's why he kept insisting on a rescue mission."

"He did?"

"Of course he did," he laughed, clasping her shoulder. "Erik convinced him to wait only long enough for him to go along." His face took on a serious edge. "Your father almost didn't survive. He wanted to go after you as soon as he woke up." He smiled. "In fact, he tried."

A smile crept across Hilde's face, imagining her father, barely off his death bed, charging through the woods to save her.

"He was in and out of delirium for over a week. When he did wake, he wanted to go after you immediately, but he couldn't even stand up. Weeks passed, and he was recovering well, but you know Erik; he decided he was ready. When the women didn't agree, he stole off into the woods to go after you on his own.

"By the time we found him, he was almost dead. In fact, we thought he was. It wasn't until we brought him back, and Annika began washing his body for the pyre, that she realized he was still alive.

"For over a week, he was unconscious. I thought he was going to die; we all did." Sigurd smiled. "But he's tough. Finally, he woke up, but for weeks after that, he'd start getting better, then worse, back and forth.

"His recovery took months before he could get out of bed and walk around. Afraid Erik would do the same thing he did the last time, my father posted a guard outside his door, and your father's friends took turns.

"Even after he had recovered, it took weeks to build his strength back up before he was fit to fight, but as soon as he was, they all set out for you. To be honest, though, it wasn't a rescue mission."

"No?"

Sigurd's tone took a solemn edge. "They went for revenge. We all thought you were dead. Only Erik believed you were still alive.

"Erik's illness is the only reason that it took so long for them to come after you. I would have come myself, but I had twisted my ankle, and Erik forbade it, certain that the woods would kill me if I weren't at my very best."

"He was right," she nodded. "If you can't get out of the way quick, you're dead."

He sighed, "I know, but I still wanted to go, and I can't help thinking that, if I'd been there ..."

As he trailed off, Hilde took his hand. "We did everything we could, Sigurd. I swear we did."

Offering a sad smile, he nodded. "I know. It's just been hard since Bridget's death, and now Father. I was supposed to go with the caravan, but Father and Mother decided they needed me to stay and help with the farm. I feel like I should have been there to protect her. Now, it's like I abandoned them both."

"You didn't abandon them," she said softly. "If you had been with the caravan, you would be dead too. Then there would be no one to look after your mother and the kids."

"I know, but at least I would have died a noble death, fighting that Beast. And who knows, maybe mine would have been the sword that killed it."

"Thor didn't kill your sister," Hilde said matter-of-factly.

Sigurd scowled. "You call it by a name?"

"I do," she insisted, "and he's no murderer."

Shaking his head, he sighed. "I heard someone say that it had cast some sort of spell over you."

She laughed. "He cast no spell. I just got to know him."

It was evident he didn't believe her, but he humored her. "And why do you say he didn't do it?"

"For one thing, at the time your sister's caravan was attacked, Thor was with me; he couldn't have done it." As he started to interrupt, she went on. "And for another, he went hunting regularly…"

"And you weren't with him," he interjected meaningfully.

"No, I wasn't but …"

"So, he could have …"

She interrupted him this time. "I saw the animals he brought home. I saw the kind of marks his claws make. They tear, Sigurd, just like a wolf's. They don't make clean slashes. He is not capable of making the precise cuts that killed my brothers and, I suspect, your sister."

He was quiet for a moment, digesting this information, then he asked, "So what are you saying?"

"I'm saying that someone else attacked the caravan and is trying to make it look like he did it. They're killing everyone so no one can tell the truth. Think about it; he's the perfect scapegoat."

"Maybe," he conceded, after a moment of thought, "or maybe you just can't see the truth of what that thing is anymore."

Hilde glared at him. "Or maybe I'm not the one who can't see the truth." Angry, she walked away and resumed her training routine.

Sigurd didn't leave; instead, he watched, and, after a few minutes, drew his sword and joined, first beside her practicing forms, then against her in what he quickly learned was full-speed sparring: his wooden sword verses her wooden axe.

As he walked her home, they talked, but the subject of the Beast did not come up again.

Over the next couple of months, Sigurd was a constant companion, always there to make her smile. Even others began to accept her, but always with a sense of reservation that she never felt from Sigurd.

"He wants to marry you," her father said at dinner one day.

Hilde smiled. "I don't think we're quite there yet, Father."

"You're not," he grunted around a mouthful of mutton, "but he is."

"What do you mean?" she asked, sensing that there was more to this than just her father's hopes.

"Are you blind, girl?" He dropped the meat and pointed a big greasy finger at her. "That boy is crazy about you. He's done everything but haul you before some witnesses by a fistful of your hair." He grinned. "Actually, that's not a bad idea."

"Father!"

"Maybe I'll mention it to him."

Fighting to keep the smile off her face, but feeling the blood rush to her cheeks, she glared at him. "You'll do no such thing. Sigurd and I are friends."

"Blind as your mother." He popped the rest of the meat into his mouth and stood up. "He'd be great for you."

Three days later, Sigurd made his true intentions clear. As they stood together in the knee-deep snow, watching the sun dip behind the horizon in a majestic display of colors, he took her hand gently in his and smiled, "Let's get married."

For a moment, Hilde only stared at him. That wasn't quite the proposal she had been hoping for, but the tenderness in his eyes melted her heart, and she nodded. "Yes, Sigurd," she smiled. "I'll marry you."

He picked her up and spun her around, then pulled her close and kissed her deeply.

The next few weeks passed at a dizzying speed in a frenzy of arrangements. She was excited but couldn't shake the sense of betrayal. Images of Thor plagued her thoughts as she tried to focus on her special day. But there was no future with Thor, she knew. Sigurd was a good, honorable man; they would have a home and children. So why did her heart ache so badly for Thor? She pushed him again from her mind. The wedding was set for the winter solstice, and, once she was married, she told herself, everything would be fine. It would be wonderful.

Finally, it was the day of her nuptials. A caravan was due that morning, bringing some of Sigurd's relatives from another clanhold. It would arrive around midday, and the wedding would follow in the afternoon. Even as Hilde dressed, putting on the dress her mother had worn to marry her father, she couldn't shake the sad bestial eyes that haunted her every thought. Part of her wanted to cancel, but she reminded herself that Thor could never be a husband to her, not in the truest sense of the word. Sigurd, on the other hand, could and would be a loving husband and father. She was determined to stay her course.

Midday came and went with no sign of the caravan, and, eventually, a group of young men went to follow the road and see why it was delayed. An hour later, the men returned. She was with Sigurd when they came charging back into the village, soaked with sweat from the hard run.

"They're dead," the leader cried. "They're all dead."

Silence. No one spoke. Time passed.

"Butchered by the Beast, just like the others."

"That's the wrong road," Hilde argued. "That's nowhere near his woods. I told you it's not him."

Women began to wail, and men cursed. "It only means it's getting bolder," Erik snarled.

"Get everyone. We'll meet in the Mead Hall," Sigurd ordered, starting away.

Hilde grabbed his sleeve. "It wasn't him," she began, but he yanked his arm free and glared at her. He was about to speak but reconsidered and stormed away.

They gathered in the Mead Hall, a grand building with broad double doors that, in pleasant weather, stood wide open, welcoming all. Dozens of torches would light the common room while a huge brazier bathed the Hall in warmth and often the sweet smell of roasting meat. It was large enough to hold the entire village, a place of community during the harsh winters, of shelter against violent storms, of celebration after a marriage or mourning after a funeral. The hall was where significant village meetings took place, and today it was full.

Men and women packed the Hall, sitting on the benches and tables. The kitchen was cold: no food or drink graced the tables today. Instead of the usual boasting, laughing, and singing, the Hall was loud with shouts and oaths of vengeance. An ominous air hung in the room, a mood of anger, hate, and murder so thick and stifling that it was hard to draw breath.

As the men argued about what to do, Yarl Kjell, the clan chief, listened for a while before raising his arm for silence. It took a moment, but the noise quieted and eventually stopped. "Unfortunately, I don't see any alternative," he began vaguely. "We've lost a lot of loved ones; we've all suffered." He turned to Sigurd. "Today was to be a day of joy for you but instead has become a day of grief. I'm sorry for you on this of all days."

Sigurd nodded his thanks but remained silent.

"Since the last attack, we closed the east road." Yarl Kjell continued. "We have done everything we could to avoid a confrontation with this monster." Many grumbled their agreement. "But we have allowed too much. It's time we stop trying to avoid this battle; it's time we take the fight to the Beast."

A deafening roar of approval erupted in the Hall.

Hilde stood near the back, but caught Sigurd's eyes and held them, silently begging him to remember what she had said.

When the uproar died down, Sigurd stood. "I'm hesitant to suggest this, but I feel it is important." Everyone was looking at him. "What if it wasn't the Beast that did ..."

Yelling and swearing cut off his last words, but one voice rose above the rest. "You've let her into your head before the knot is even tied," Erik chided.

Other men laughed, but Sigurd stood his ground. "She presents a good case," he continued, but again was drowned out by yelling. This time, he went on, shouting to be heard. "Blades, not claws, killed my kin."

"Enough!" Kjell yelled, silencing the room. "This monster has been a threat looming over our heads for twenty years, and I have no doubt of its guilt. It's high time we eliminate this menace altogether."

Again, the room erupted in a roar of approval.

"And what will you do?" Hilde screamed, with fire in her eyes. "Will you march an army into the woods to be swallowed whole?" She glared at her chieftain. "We lost three warriors, three brave warriors, the last time that was tried."

"Silence your woman, Sigurd," Kjell demanded.

"As a shield maiden, she has earned her voice," he replied.

Hilde sneered at Kjell. "If you want them to go off and die, then surely you'll lead them."

There was silence for a moment. The challenge loomed, and the whole Hall waited for an answer. At last, Kjell nodded. "Of course, I'll lead them."

"Lead an army into that woods," Sigurd warned him, "and you'll be dead by sundown."

"They're right," Erik agreed. "The woods will swallow us whole."

Many who had been with Erik and Ilya the last time nodded and voiced their agreement.

"Then we will not send an army," Kjell announced. "Instead, we'll enter the woods one and two at a time at intervals. The woods won't know we're an army. Then, on the other side, we'll regroup for the attack."

Hilde left the Hall while the men were still ironing out the details. Their plan could work, she thought, making her way home. There she stripped off the gown and pulled on her leather jerkin and boots. She moved with purpose, fastening her belt, tying on her axe, and hefting her crossbow with one intent; she had to get to Thor before they did.

"Where do you think you're going," Erik asked, entering the cottage just as she was leaving.

She hesitated for just a moment before responding. "You know where I'm going. I have to."

Taking a step toward her, Erik's eyes narrowed. "I'm not going to let you warn him." He reached for her, but she was faster. She spun away, then kicked him off balance and ran out the door. He gave chase, but her light feet quickly outdistanced him.

"I knew you'd try this," Sigurd said, stepping into view between her and the woods' edge.

She slowed down. "You can't stop me," she said defiantly, unconsciously fingering her axe's handle.

"I could try," he offered with a sad smile, "but I won't."

As he stepped aside, she eyed him carefully and walked past him. "Thank you."

She stepped into the trees and heard him one last time. "I could have loved you."

"I know," she whispered to herself, as she trudged through the snow, plunging deeper into the woods. The sun would be going down soon, and she had no desire to get caught in this place after dark. Focusing more on the sky than on her surroundings, she hurried toward the castle. Vines entangled her feet, but a swift swing of her axe set her free again, and she continued. She was frustrated by branches and tripped up by undergrowth and mud but refused to let anything stop or even slow her. This time, constantly eying the sky, the trip was a much shorter one, and, just as the sun was reaching the horizon, she burst out along the old road.

As she ran past the old broken gate, a shadow darkened the window in the pink room. Charging past the rose garden and up the front stone steps, she burst through the door and took the stairs to the second floor two at a time, yelling at the top of her lungs. "Thor!" She pounded down the hall and shoved open the door to his private sanctuary. "Thor! They're coming!"

Sitting on the couch, staring at the rose with a single petal, Thor said nothing.

"Didn't you hear me?" she asked, out of breath, with her hands on her knees. "I said they're coming. They're coming through the woods one at a time to trick it, but they're all coming to kill you."

He looked up then, slowly. "It doesn't matter." A sad smile crossed his face. "But I'm glad you came."

"Of course it matters," she snapped. "How can you say that?"

"It just doesn't matter anymore," he repeated, and just as the words left his mouth, the last, lonely petal broke free and began floating slowly to the floor. He watched it.

"It does matter, Thor!" she yelled at him. "I came back to help because I love you."

The petal landed softly on the floor.

Tears ran down his furry face as he looked sadly from the petal to her. "If only you'd come sooner."

"What?" she asked confused. "What do you mean? I came as soon as I ..."

The fallen petal flared brilliantly with a blinding pink flash. When she opened her eyes again, there before her, Hilde saw not a rose but a woman surrounded by a glowing pink aura. She was beautiful; her long honey-brown hair framed a gentle heart-shaped face. She was no taller than Hilde but regal. Her clear blue eyes spoke of kindness and sincerity, of purity of spirit and strength of will.

"Mother?" Thor cried out in wonder.

She smiled lovingly at her son, then turned to Hilde. "You love Thor?"

Hilde nodded, then found her voice. "I do."

"Even though he looks like this?"

Turning to look at him, she smiled. "Yes, I love him.'

"I know he told you about what happened and about the curse," she said, "but he never told you how it could be broken."

Hilde's head snapped back to her. "Broken?"

"It could have been if you had confessed your love for Thor before the last petal fell."

Tears streaming from her eyes, she cried, "Why didn't you tell me?"

"It had to be a true confession of love," Queen Gerta explained. "If he had told you, your compassion might have interfered."

Looking at the floor where the last petal had fallen, she wept, "But now I'm too late."

"You are too late to break the curse," the queen confirmed. "But curses are funny things."

"Funny things?" Hilde asked, a hint of hope in her voice.

"Curses and their cures depend on the words that are spoken in casting them," she explained cryptically. "The goddess Frigg granted my prayer and gave Thor a way to break the curse, but only if he found true love before the last petal fell to the floor."

"I heard your confession of love, and so did Frigg," she explained. "You spoke the words after the petal fell but before it landed on the floor. Magic depends on words, and in this one, there is some vagary." She smiled. "Some ... wiggle room."

"Wiggle room?" Hilde and Thor asked together. They looked at each other and Hilde smiled. "So, you can break it."

The queen shook her head. "Sadly, no. It can't be broken, but it can be altered."

"Altered?" they again asked in unison.

The older woman became very solemn. "Hilde, if you choose to, you may share his curse."

"No!" Thor yelled, aghast, jumping to his feet.

Hilde looked at Thor, then back to his mother. "What do you mean?"

"Forget it," Thor snapped before anything more could be said.

Hilde spun and shoved him. It was like pushing a tree, but it made her point. "You don't tell me to forget it." She glared at him, then turned back to the queen expectantly.

The older woman was smiling, but the smile withered. "If you accept the goddess' offer, then you will both be human except for the three nights of the full moon. For those nights, you will both be transformed into this," she indicated Thor.

"No!" Thor pleaded with her, turning Hilde to face him. "You can't do this. Please think about it. You don't want to be a monster. This is my burden to bear."

"Do you love me?" she asked him.

"More than anything."

"Well, I love you too."

"Then don't do this."

Smiling, she stroked the soft fur of his face. "People who love each other share the bad as well as the good."

"But ..."

Hilde gently pinched his lips shut and turned to the queen. "I accept."

"So mote it be."

Immediately the evening's quiet was shattered by his preternatural screams and the sounds of breaking bones. Thor's body jerked one way, then another. He fell to the floor and screamed as the magic ran its course, breaking and twisting him until he lost consciousness. As soon as the transformation was complete, Hilde knelt and cradled his head in her lap as tears streamed down her face. His chest rose and fell, so she knew he was alive. Sweat soaked the long brown hair that framed his chiseled face, with high cheekbones and a strong jaw. A thin brown mustache grew over his soft pink lips. Hilde admired his tall, muscular build, even dwarfed as it was by the Beast's enormous clothes. When his eyes fluttered open, she gazed down into his deep brown eyes, so full of warmth and love.

When he regained consciousness, as he lay on the floor in a pool of sweat, he felt his head lifted and propped up, and fingers tenderly wiping his face. Opening his eyes, for the first time Thor saw the woman he loved with his own human eyes. Fiery red curls cascaded over her shoulders and tickled his now human cheeks. And those eyes … before they had been just another shade of gray, but now, for the first time, he was transfixed by those bright emerald orbs. "You're beautiful."

A smile spread over her tear-soaked face as she held him and lovingly rocked him in her arms. "So are you."

For a moment, they simply gazed into each other's eyes; then Thor turned to his mother. "Are you …?"

She was gone. In her place stood again a single pink rose in full bloom. Its petals were restored, and it stood glowing and slowly rotating once more, seeming to radiate her love and pride.

A pang of sadness and loss washed over Thor as he stared at the symbol of his mother's sacrifice.

"Look." Hilde pointed out the window. "Look at the woods."

Rising to his feet beside her, Thor saw what she meant. The cursed woods that had grown up around the castle was turning to ash and blowing away in the evening's wind. "It's over," he whispered softly, squeezing her hand.

"Not yet, it's not." She indicated a dozen armed men just outside the castle gate and nearly half that again walking toward them through where the woods had been.

"Come on." Thor ran from the pink room, down the hall to his old bedroom, where the stone woman still occupied the bed. Without a word, he opened the wardrobe and pulled out some of his old clothes.

"What are you doing?" Hilde asked, confused.

He spared her only a brief glance before returning to his search. "I can't go out there and face down a kill squad dressed like this." He tugged at the oversized clothes that now hung on his much smaller frame. Finally satisfied with his scrounging, Thor pulled off the oversized clothes. Although much smaller than the Beast, he was still a large man. His body had not aged during the curse, but still possessed the hard, corded muscles, honed by years hunting in the dark woods.

Donning the clothes he had chosen, he caught Hilde staring at him with a quirky little smile. "What?"

"Nothing," she grinned. "Just looking ... at how different you are."

He smiled. "Good different, I hope."

"Eh." She bounced her head side to side non-committally.

Thor stepped forward and wrapped his arms around her. "I love you, Hilde. I love you so much."

"I love you too," she said, hugging him back. "And I love the new look."

Drawing back, he caught her eyes with his and held them. "I can't thank you enough," he whispered, his eyes glistening with unshed tears of gratitude. "You don't know ..."

Pressing her lips to his, she silenced him with a long loving kiss, then smiled. "I do know. Now let's go see your visitors."

"Our visitors," he corrected her, fastening the last few buttons as they left the room. Thor led the way to a room that he had never shown Hilde. Opened with a key, the old ironbound door creaked.

"The armory," Hilde whispered. "I've never seen so many weapons in one place."

Wordlessly, Thor continued through to another door in the back of the armory, which he again opened with a key. Inside he found, just ashe remembered, the private armory for the king and his bodyguards.

"That's your armor?" she asked, amazed by the gilded scale mail.

He nodded. "It was my father's," he explained, hoisting the padded tunic off the stand and over his head. "Now it's mine." Hilde immediately moved to help with the fastenings as piece after piece found its place until Thor looked every bit the warrior king. After buckling the sword belt around his waist, he picked up the crowned helmet and glanced around. "There were no shield maidens in my father's bodyguard, but something might fit you, if you want it." Before she could reply, he continued, "I hope it doesn't come to a fight, and if it does, I want you to stay out of it, but …"

"Stay out of it?" she repeated angrily. "We're in this together."

"Somehow I was afraid you might say that." He squeezed her shoulder. "Like I said, I hope it doesn't come to a fight, but, either way, I want you safe." He reached for a scale breastplate.

"I can't fight in that," she laughed, waving it off and grabbing a coat of chainmail. "Even this will be heavy," she smiled, "but I like it."

In mere minutes, the two were making their way through the Grand Foyer and out into the cold evening air. In the courtyard, among the mysterious pink roses, stood the "army," a score of men armed with axes, swords, and even a pitchfork. They all looked quietly at him and each other.

"Where's the Beast?" one man called from the crowd.

"Who's in charge here?" Thor demanded in his best kingly voice.

One man stepped forward and removed his helmet. "Is that you, Thor?"

"Kjell?"

"You don't look like I remember," the chieftain said, fingering the hilt of his sword.

"Don't I?"

Kjell's eyes narrowed. "You look human."

"I am human." He stared at the mass of men. "Hilde has broken the curse." Then he commanded Kjell. "Stand down."

"Broken or not, what you did under the curse cannot be forgotten." Kjell glared at him. "Murder is murder."

Standing his ground, Thor looked steadily at the older man. "Even as the Beast, I never lost my faculties. Only my physical form was transformed; inwardly, I have always been me."

"Then you condemn yourself," Kjell growled, drawing his sword. "You admit your guilt."

"I did not kill your loved ones," Thor declared quickly to the assembly. "I never hurt anyone who wasn't here to hurt me."

"You lie!" someone yelled from the crowd.

"I'm not lying," he countered, then looked back at Kjell. "As the Beast, my claws were no different than a beast. They did not slice, they ripped. Whoever attacked those caravans wanted people to think it was me, but it wasn't. Have a look around. You won't find any of the booty here. I'm innocent."

"You could have hidden it somewhere." Kjell accused.

Thor decided to change tactics. "You were one of my father's bodyguards," he said with a hard edge to his voice. "You swore an oath to protect and defend the king and the royal family." The words stung the older man, and Thor's voice grew louder. "To protect, defend and obey the Blood."

"That's over," Kjell shouted. "It's all over. The kingdom is gone. The oath doesn't matter."

"It's not gone," Thor shouted back. "The crown prince stands before you now." His voice became low and menacing. "I wonder if your oath means as little to Odin as it does to you."

For a moment, there was only silence. Then Kjell donned his helmet, lifted his sword, and advanced a few steps. "The kingdom is gone. I'm Yarl now."

Thor smiled. "That's it, isn't it, Kjell. You know I didn't kill those people."

"I ..."

Thor's shout cut off what he was going to say. "It isn't about them, is it? It's not about righteous vengeance or honor or duty or oath. It's about power."

With a scream, Kjell charged and swung his sword. Thor barely had time to clear the scabbard with his sword and raise it to block the vicious blow. He spun to the left and faced off against his opponent. "Let the gods judge us!" He blocked a second downward strike and countered, slashing at his opponent's right side, but Kjell parried with ease.

"Kill him," Kjell yelled to his men, delivering another blow that clinked off Thor's armor.

With a grunt of pain, the prince lunged at the older man's abdomen. His sword scraped the armor but was knocked aside before finding its mark.

Men began to move, and Thor prepared to meet the new threat, but Hilde called out loud and clear. "The gods will judge these men!" She raised her axe. "And I'll cut down any man who interferes."

Thor sidestepped Kjell's thrust and spun to deliver a solid hit to the chieftain's armored side.

He glanced at Hilde, who stood facing Kjell's warriors, her attention divided between them and his own fight for his life. The distraction cost him as Kjell brought his sword down hard on the prince's armored left shoulder.

"As will I," a young man said, stepping up beside her.

"And I."

Thorsen glanced over to see Erik pushing through the men to stand with her. No one else made any move to interfere as the single combat raged.

Thor stepped back hurriedly to avoid a wide slash, then stepped in behind the arc to deliver a fierce blow to Kjell's head. The blow slammed into his helmet, sending Kjell staggering backward. Using the sword's momentum, Thor swung around and drove the blade as hard as he could, aiming for the old bodyguard's helmeted head. Kjell saw it at the last moment and tried to move, but it was too late. The blade landed with a dull thud. The helmet buckled under the mighty blow, caving into his skull, and a flow of blood streamed down the Yarl's face. His legs turned to jelly, and he collapsed in a boneless heap. Just to be sure, Thor plunged his blade deep into Kjell's eye socketuntil it slammed to a stop at the back of the skull.

Standing over the dead chieftain, Thor turned to scan the scene around him. Hilde stood, with her axe in hand and a fierce smile on her lips. Beside her was a tall, broad young man with a sword and shield. His attention, however, was drawn to the band of men around them, who appeared uncertain whether to attack an enemy or kneel to a king.

With no concern for the blood and gore, Hilde stepped over Kjell's body and fell to one knee in the crimson snow. "My king!"

For a moment, there was only silence. Then the young man who had stood beside her dropped to one knee. "Hail, King Thor!"

Erik followed suite, and, as if that were the cue they needed, the rest of the men took a knee. "Hail, King Thor!"

Pulling Hilde gently to her feet, Thor hugged her and smiled. "Queen Hilde." She kissed him; then they turned together to face the men.

"You look familiar," Thor said, offering his hand to the young man who had stood beside Hilde and had been the first man there to proclaim him king.

"Sigurd, My Lord, son of Ilya. My father proudly served in the king's army, and if you'll have me, I'll proudly serve in yours."

Thor nodded, "I remember your father well, a good man and a fierce warrior. It will be an honor to have his son fight at my side. How fares your father? Is he here?" he asked, scanning the gathered faces.

"No, Sire." Sigurd answered sadly. "The woods killed him last summer."

Thor glanced at Hilde, whose slight nod confirmed his suspicions. He turned back to the young man. "I'm sorry for your loss, truly a loss to all of us."

"Thank you, Sire," Sigurd turned to Hilde, a weak smile on his lips. "My queen."

Before she could respond, the distant sounds of battle drew everyone's attention.

Turning, Thor saw a village boy running toward them, yelling for Yarl Kjell.

"What is it, Gerd?" Hilda asked.

"A fort!" Gerd called, pointing in the direction of the distant din of battle.

"Fort?"

Closing the gap, Gerd slowed, panting. "There's a ... fort in the woods ... off the East Road .... Old Carl ... he refused to wait ... He led an attack."

"Sire?" someone called

Remembering the training from his youth, Thor called out "Form ranks!" As the men, unaccustomed to organized movement, tried to fall into some semblance of order, he walked to the front. "March!" Hilde took her place on his right, with Sigurd to his left, as he led his little army through the sparse snow-covered forest where the dark woods had stood for so many years. A march that would have taken hours took less than half an hour.

When they reached the scene of the battle, off the East Road and just inside where the dark woods had been, they saw a small fort. Its walls were well-constructed, with upright logs, twice the height of a man, tightly bound together and painted with black lines to blend into the surrounding dark wood. With the woods gone, however, the camouflaged walls now stood in stark contrast to their new surroundings. It had become visible when the curse was broken and the woods disappeared. Now visible also were some of the spoils and trophies recently stolen from caravans. A band of brigands and highwaymen fought to defend their lair from the besieging villagers.

Mere boys and old men and women, those who had remained in the village, were now locked in mortal combat with a band of brigands. These mothers, brothers, and fathers of the dead, of those butchered on the East Road, fought with ferocity, a madness beyond the ken of a sane man. For so long, they had lived in terror, in the shadow of a nightmare. So many deaths had, for so long, gone unavenged. They fought on pure passion and righteous rage; there was no thought, only madness; there was no pain, only fury; there was no fear, only abandon. The villagers had numbers and madness, but the brigands had vastly superior skill. Bodies littered the ground; for every brigand, two or three villagers lay dead or wounded.

Upon seeing Thor's 'army' approaching, the brigands shouted at one another and disengaged the villagers to run back to the safety of their fort. Almost immediately, brigands on the walls loosed arrows and bolts at the surrounding villagers who hurried back out of range, carrying or dragging wounded family and friends.

After quietly surveying the scene before him, Thor turned to Sigurd. "Tell them to stop attacking. Take positions around the fort so no one can get out, but stay out of range of their weapons." As Sigurd hurried to follow his instructions, Thor turned to Hilde. "Take some men and gather all the bows and crossbows you can find and distribute them evenly around the fort. If anyone makes a break for it, open fire. No one leaves that fort."

Turning, Hilde called out a few names and relayed the orders. She, however, remained at his side. "We aren't going to be able to shoot into the fort very well. The archers may be able to cut down any who try to escape, but we need to attack." She looked around. "The people are enraged; they want revenge."

"I know, and they'll have it," Thor promised as two men approached from the mob of villagers.

The older of the two, a tall round man with short silver hair, squinted into the dim light and smiled. "The gods be praised; it's him!"

"How can you be sure?" the younger man of markedly similar features asked suspiciously. "It's been twenty years."

The older man looked at the younger as if he were daft. "I'd know that face after twenty years as surely as I'd know yours." As he drew close, he dropped to one knee. "For twenty years, we prayed for you to return, Sire." He grabbed his son and pulled him down beside himself. "My son and I are at your service."

"I'm honored," Thor smiled, offering his hand and, with some effort, pulling the corpulent older man to his feet. "You are most welcome."

"I fought with your father." Looking down at himself, he smiled wryly. Well, I'm not the same spry young man I was then, but the best day of my life was when the king singled me out for holding the bridge …"

"I remember you," Thor interrupted, smiling. "Ivar, right? You single-handedly defended the bridge on the king's flank and essentially won the battle by yourself."

Standing a little taller, Ivar beamed with pride as a tear trickled down his cheek. "Not single-handedly, Sire. Many good men gave their lives to defend that bridge; I happened to be the one to survive it."

"I'm very honored to have you and your son"—Thor said, nodding to the younger man—"at my side today."

Ivar indicated his son, "Ingvar, my oldest; he can fight."

"I have no doubt." Thor nodded to the younger man.

Ivar turned to the fort. "These murderers butchered our friends and families and made it look like the …" he hesitated.

"Like I had done it," Thor finished for him.

"Aye, Sire." He hung his head. "And I'm ashamed to admit that they fooled me."

"There's no shame in reaching the most obvious conclusion. They went to great lengths to make you all believe it was me. But I never lost my mind, and I never hurt anyone who wasn't trying to hurt me."

Thor paused. "That fort looks pretty well built; if we attack, their archers will cut us down."

"We could do it," Ingvar insisted.

"I'm sure we could, but we'd lose a lot of good men." Thor considered his options. "They can't have much for supplies in there. We could starve them out."

"No!" Ivar growled. "I mean, I don't think the people will wait that long. They need their revenge."

"He's right," Hilde agreed. "These people won't stand for a long, drawn out siege. Too many have died."

Thor thought for a moment, then asked, "Ivar, how much oil do you have in the village, for lamps and torches?"

Ivar grinned. "Like father, like son," he nodded. "The Battle of the Crooked Gorge."

Thor's eyes became hard and cold. Without another word, Ivar turned, pulling his son along, to get the oil.

"The Battle of Crooked Gorge?" Hilde asked, unfamiliar with the name.

"It was the first time I accompanied my father into battle, the first time I understood the savagery of war."

He fell silent. Old Carl, with tears in his eyes and pain in his heart, led a steady stream—young, old, and everywhere in between—to present themselves to the returned king, to swear allegiance and welcome him back. Some had served his father, others had only heard the stories of the good old days, but all wanted to help restore their kingdom to its former glory.

As soon as the weapons arrived, archers and crossbowmen took up positions as he had instructed, assuring no escape for the besieged brigands. After only a short time, Ivar and his sons returned with carts carrying dozens of clay jars containing villager's oil supply, and as much linen as could be gathered on short notice.

"Plug the ends of the jars with soaked linen," Thor commanded.

Hilde turned on him, wide-eyed. "You're going to burn the fort, burn them alive?" A cry of pain drew her attention to a village boy with a brigand's arrow in his stomach. Her eyes hardened, and Thor knew she was thinking of her own brothers. Her face was a mask of cold hatred as she looked back to the fort. "Do it! Burn them!"

They remained silent and watched as the preparations were made, watched as the jars were hurled by slings to shatter against the fort, the rags clinging to its walls which ran with thick dark oil.

"Archers!" Thor called, and his archers raised their bows with flaming arrows. "Ready!"

Yelling could be heard from the fort, terrified pleas and cries of surrender. Men begged for mercy as their victims had begged and pleaded for their own lives.

"Loose!" Thor cried out, dropping his arm and watching a rain of fire sail through the dark night air, igniting the fort into an inferno that lit the now sparse woods as if it were high noon.

Men screamed and ran from the fort, only to be skewered by the villager's arrows or cut down by their unforgiving blades. Blood-curdling screams of terror and dying filled the air as Thor and Hilde, the new king and queen-to-be, looked on. As the cloud of smoke, carrying the stench of roasted flesh, rose into the sky, it turned the nearly full moon blood-red. To Thor, who knew well what the full moon would bring, its color tonight stood in the sky as a harbinger of things to come.

The inferno raged late into the night. It wasn't until the horizon was on fire with the rising sun that Thor and Hilde walked among the charred, smoldering remains of the brigands and their fort. Among the cinders and ashes were found items stolen from the caravans and horrific four-bladed weapons that the murderers had used to frame the Beast. Their dead were granted no honors; their remains were left lying in the mud and ashes as carrion for birds and beasts.

Not until the sun neared its apex did Thor and Hilde return to the castle. They lit a fire in the hearth and curled up together, alone once again.

"What are we going to tell them?" Hilde asked, comfortably nestled in Thor's arms, her head laid on his chest, listening to the beating of his heart.

"I've been thinking about that," he said, then fell silent.

She lifted her head to look up at him. "We can't exactly tell them that we turn into monsters every full moon." When he didn't respond, she asked, "Can we?"

He smiled and hugged her. "Somehow, I don't think they'd understand."

"Me neither." A moment of silence passed before she said, "Frigg blessed us by breaking the curse." He shifted, and she could feel his eyes on her as she snuggled back against his chest. "What if we go into seclusion for three nights and two days every full moon to devote ourselves completely to honoring her?

"Hmm." He absently twirled his fingers into her fiery red hair. "Actually, that's pretty good."

"We could close ourselves up in the North Wing, leaving instructions that we are not to be disturbed."

Thor laughed.

"What?"

"Instructions for a king not to be disturbed last only until something happens that someone thinks is important enough to interrupt the king. We might get a day. No, the only way to make it work is if we spent that time outside the castle and gave someone the power to act on our authority in the event of a crisis."

"But we could make it work," she said hopefully.

Without lifting her head, she could hear the smile in his voice. "We could." His voice became serious. "But we would have to trust someone, trust him with our secret. He would have to understand the authority he has and why he has it. Otherwise, we'd find someone coming into the forest to look for us, someone with something so important it couldn't wait."

Silence hung heavy; the only sound was a crackling fire a few feet away. Moments passed before Hilde spoke. "We turn tomorrow night."

The next morning, they ate breakfast together. It was quiet until Thor said, "I've seen the way Sigurd looks at you."

Hilde's head snapped up. "He's loyal to king and country."

"I'm not questioning his loyalty." His gentle smile allayed her fears.

"He loves me," she admitted, watching his reaction. "We were supposed to be married on the day that I came back to you." When he didn't speak, she felt the need to explain. "I didn't think we could be together. I thought ..."

"It's okay," he smiled. "I understand." He reached up and stroked her cheek. "I'd given up hope. I never imagined I would ever be a man again."

"Sigurd grew up on Ilya's stories of fighting in your father's army. Ilya instilled in Sigurd a sense of honor and duty. Yes, he loves me." She looked intently into his eyes. "He will love me as his queen, and he will honor you as his king. Despite his feelings for me—or maybe because of them—I would entrust our lives into his hands without a second thought."

Thor nodded. "I knew Ilya. He wasn't much older than I was. If Sigurd is half the man his father was, then I believe that we can trust him."

"We can."

"With our secret?"

Her answer was immediate and emphatic. "Yes."

The wedding was to be a lavish affair. Envoys were dispatched to all the clanholds of the kingdom with news that the gods had found favor with Prince Thor and broken the curse, restoring him to his proper place. They carried word that the celebration was open to all, regardless of station. Nobles and commoners alike were welcome to attend and stand witness to the royal nuptials and partake in the three days of festivities.

The castle was a work in progress. Repairing the damage from two decades of neglect would take months, but now, during this time of joy and unity, its halls rang with merriment and laughter.

The wedding and coronation were held in the courtyard, where, despite the frozen, snow-covered ground, pink roses still glowed in full bloom, a testament to the tribulations this kingdom had endured and overcome. It was said that these extraordinary roses were a manifestation of the esteem in which the gods held the royal couple, and that, as long as they bloomed, they would stand as proof that the royal line was favored by the gods.

After the coronation, in the rose courtyard, another ceremony took place. Feuds were set aside, offenses were forgiven, as, one by one, the yarls in attendance, who had ruled a divided nation, knelt and swore fealty to their rightful king and queen. Thus began a new age of unity and harmony throughout the land.

Not all the yarls had answered the crown prince's summons or attended the festivities. Some refused to accept King Thor's authority, refused to recognize the oaths they had once sworn to his father. They had tasted power and were loath to put it down. The yarls in attendance, loyal to the crown, cried out for war, but King Thor was a voice of reason and calm, insisting that it was not their place to hold men accountable for their oaths and that Odin would judge them.

Indeed, it came to pass, as full moons came and went and the seasons changed, that the royal couple's pious devotion was said to have earned the blessings of the gods and that Odin himself smote their enemies. The oath-breaking yarls were found in pools of their own blood, torn to pieces by the wolves of Valhalla.

Less than a year after Thor's and Hilde's marriage and coronation, Queen Hilde gave birth to their first child: a beautiful baby girl. As the sun set on the first full moon of her young life, in the nursery lit only by the magical glow of her grandmother's essence, Princess Else screamed as her bones began to break.

www.ingramcontent.com/pod-product-compliance
Lightning Source LLC
Chambersburg PA
CBHW030206130726
47898CB00012B/906